Marji's Books

The Christmas Tree Treasure Hunt

Grime Fighter Series

Grime Beat

Grime Wave

Grime Spree

Grime Family

Grime & Punishment

Heath's Point Suspense

Counter Point

Breaking Point

Boiling Point (coming soon)

Flash Point (coming soon)

Dallas Duets Clean Billionaire Romance

Ain't Misbehaving

Cry Me a River (coming soon)

Puttin' on the Ritz (coming soon)

Grime & Punishment

Grime Fighter Mystery
Book #5

Marji Laine

Grime & Punishment
Second Edition
© 2019 Marji Laine
ISBN: 978-1-944120-96-2

Faith Driven Book Production Services
Find out more about the author: *Marji Laine.com*
Or email her at: *AuthorMarjiLaine@gmail.com*

Printed in the United States of America.

I dedicate this book to my first born,
Richard.
He has been a great inspiration for these
stories.
(That can be a terribly dangerous statement
when speaking about murder mysteries.)
But his inspiration hasn't been the deadly
kind.
He has the same type of humor that my
main characters, particularly Jay and Cal
carry throughout the story.

I'm so thankful to you, Boy,
for the laughter,
the encouragement,
and for the delightful new daughter,
your amazing wife,
that you've brought into our lives.

I love you, bigtime!

Be imitators of God, therefore,
as dearly loved children
and live a life of love
just as Christ loved us
and gave His life up for us
as a fragrant offering and
sacrifice to God.
Ephesians 5:13, 15-16 NIV

Chapter One

Dani Foster munched on the last caramel Bugle chip like any twenty-something out with her favorite guy and tried to forget she was a Judas with a target on her back. Pulling her knees under her chin, she leaned against Jay's strong shoulder where he'd propped himself against the trunk of a tree. The cars on the busy road beneath them kept up a constant white noise.

Jay Hunter leaned close. "Want to walk off our dinner?" His warm breath tickled her ear.

Whatever you say. She shouldn't be so infatuated with this man. No, her feelings had gone way past infatuation months ago. In a perfect world, the two of them might actually have a chance of forever. But her world was far from perfect.

He pulled her to her feet and held her close. She let his half-smile capture her attention and let the moment linger until the raucous screeching of some bird interrupted her reverie. The most annoying sound worked perfectly as a ring tone for the most annoying person she knew. She shut her eyes and reached for her phone. No use in trying to ignore it, and doing so could put her and Jay both at risk.

She gave Jay and apologetic grimace. He didn't know everything, but he'd had to deal with her calls from Matthew Donaldson before. She swiped the screen. "You've got lousy timing, Matt." She took a few steps away from Jay, leaning against a tree to keep her balance on the steep incline.

"And you've got a lousy memory." Her witness protection agent had a sharp edge to his voice. "What happened to my instructions that you should contact me before leaving your apartment?"

Of course. Only one time in over a week that she had left without his permission, and he threw a fit. She lowered her voice to a whispered as she backed away a few more feet. "It's not like you aren't tracking me through my phone."

"Exactly. Stay there. I'm coming for you."

She caught Jay's eye and mouthed *I'm sorry* before turning her back. "Not exactly convenient timing right now."

"Not for me either, thank you very much. I'll meet you at the parking lot of Flag Pole Hill in twenty minutes." He clicked off.

"Wait! What?" She was speaking to no one at this point. He was coming here? What was the man thinking? That would mean she'd have to explain everything to Jay.

"Ready to walk?" He tucked the rolled blanket into his trunk and shut the lid.

"Absolutely." She'd have a good fifteen minutes to explain things gently. Well, as much as she was willing to share. She wasn't ready for him to completely hate her.

"I've been wanting to bring you back here for a while. Remember our first date?" He reached for her hand and helped her down the slope toward an easier path that would lead them back toward the way they had come.

"This is a perfect evening." Or it would be if the impending visit from Matt and the looming explanation didn't blot out her attempts to relish every moment with this man she adored.

"Hard to believe so much has happened since then."

So much. She'd almost lost him. The memory burned through her.

"I hope, now that you've quit your job at Kellerman's, you'll stay out of so many dangerous situations." He paused at the grassy shoreline.

Kellerman Crisis and Trauma Cleaners hadn't had anything to do with the events of the past several months. In truth, crime scene cleaning was tedious and would've been downright boring if she hadn't had her imagination weaving together stories about what she found on the job.

And as for putting herself into anymore danger, Matt had threatened to have her locked up. "I'm behaving." She stifled a chuckle as her five-year-old self said *I'm being-have* in her mind. Her nerves were letting in goofy thoughts. She fisted her one empty hand and braced herself to give a full explanation of her secrets.

"Good." He pulled her close. "I don't want to lose you. I've already been close to that, and I never want to go through it again." He stooped slightly and kissed her forehead. "You're precious to me, Dani. I can't imagine life without you." He took a step back. "And I want you to always be part of my life."

Still grasping one of her hands, he slowly lowered to one knee.

No. No. No. He couldn't be doing this. Not now with what she was about to tell him.

"Dani Foster." His gaze clung to hers and refused release.

Lord, this is going to break him. Why, why had she ever allowed herself to get serious with him in the first place. She was playing around with this man's heart, with his life.

"I want you to be my wife." He held up a solitaire that caught the moonlight and sparkled.

Okay, she hadn't been playing, but she'd known this relationship would never last. Not once he knew the depth of her depravity.

"Will you marry me?"

She realized that her mouth had been hanging open slightly. She shut it without moving her gaze. Jay waited for an answer. An answer she wanted desperately to give. Didn't she have the right to happiness? After all, she'd given up her entire life, everything she loved from photography to going to church. Why did she have to give up still more?

"This is where you leap into my arms with a loud *yes* and plant a big kiss on my lips." His eyebrows raised and his grin grew.

The squeal of brakes and slamming car doors on the ridge above them startled her. "Are you sure she's here?" A man's voice. One she knew far too well.

"This is where the tracker led us. She has to be here."

Robert had found her.

Jay tried to read Dani's expression. Normally, he had no trouble seeing every thought pass over her eyes. He'd expected the surprise, but the terror that filled them was a little disconcerting. She lifted her gaze to the ridge behind him. Was she trying to quell tears or something?

A rock bit into his knee. "Honey, did you hear me?" Why wasn't she even looking at the ring he extended?

"Shhh." She looked down at him again. Her face pale. She glanced at the ring and shook her head. Backing up a few steps, she looked up to the ridge again and beckoned at him to follow her.

What was going on?

She put her finger to her lips, though Jay already sensed her caution. A couple of men were up there talking about baseball. At least, it sounded like that. Something about a third strike, but most of what they said he couldn't make out.

Dani reached for his hand and tugged, leading him toward the trees. The steeper trail was downright treacherous in the dark. He should have argued, but the moonlight was bright enough. And the look on her face had spoken volumes. Whatever or whoever was on that ridge frightened his girl. He felt for his weapon, just touching it for reassurance.

"What are you waiting for? Find..." The shout was unmistakably angry.

Dani's grip on his hand tightened, and she broke into a trot under the cover of the tree line. He followed for a couple of minutes until the trail turned right toward the highway below them. Dani didn't know the layout of this park nearly as well as he did. He pulled her to the left cutting over to a different path, not as covered by trees, but one that would lead them to the corner where his station of the Dallas Police Department was 100 yards across a busy intersection and another tree covered field.

"I can't." Her harsh whisper broke through the melody of cicadas and the fading rhythm of the shallow waves. "I have someone who is meeting me."

What was she talking about? "Are you trying to avoid those men on the ridge or me?"

"No, Jay. You don't understand." She glanced at the approaching cars then looked back over her shoulder into the dark trees.

Though he hadn't wanted to think much about it, he understood more than she thought. She was obviously under some sort of protection. He'd already surmised her predicament. That was why she always had to call some *friend of the family*.

And why his own captain skirted his questions, finally telling him to can-it.

He pointed to the lighted windows of the station barely peeking through the trees. "It's a short jog, Hon. Then, you can collect yourself and call whomever you need to call. And maybe..."

A car screeched to a halt at the curb next to them.

Dani jumped. Jay reached for his gun, stepping in front of her and pushed her backward.

The window rolled down. "Get in, now. Sorry, hero. Only room for one."

Jay didn't move but gripped the gun. Next to him, Dani released a broad exhale. "It's all right." She took a step toward the car.

"Wait a minute. What's going on?" And who was the blond superhero with perfect teeth in the driver's seat?

She opened the passenger side. "I'm sorry, Jay. I can't explain."

Jay gripped the frame of the door, like he could actually force the car to stay in place. No words came, though. He'd laid his heart out already.

Dani hesitated and stepped back to him,

wrapping her arms around his neck. "I do love you."

"Then, what is this?"

She backed away, locking her gaze with his. "Goodbye, Jay."

Without another word or a backward glance, she slipped into the seat and the car took off, making the right turn and merging into traffic.

Goodbye. Heartless. Hopeless. Final.

Jay looked back toward the park he'd just evacuated. Who were the men talking and why had Dani darted like a hunted rabbit? For a brief second, Jay started to return to his car and get some answers. Then he whirled. No. Someone else had all the answers he needed, and he was determined to get every one of them.

Jay practically ran to the cube he shared with Calvin Cutter. "I need the truth." He hadn't meant to attack his former partner, but the edge in his voice revealed the frustration he'd harbored when Cal learned the truth about Dani. A truth that neither he nor the captain had been willing to share.

Until now.

The older man lifted his hands over his graying head in mock surrender and shifted the ever-present toothpick from one side of his mouth to the other. "Okay, I did it. Put me away, copper."

"No joke, Cal." Jay lowered his voice to a growl. "Dani just ran for her life from someone on the hill."

Cal half-stood and slipped his phone from his desk to his pocket. "What happened to her?"

Jay raked his hand through his short hair. "She got in the car with some guy who drove off." How could he have just let her go like that?

"What guy?"

"Someone she knew." His mind's eye retraced the moment. "No one captured her or anything. She said goodbye..." Like a forever goodbye. He gave himself another mental kick.

Cal removed his phone from his pocket and laid it on the desk before settling back into his creaking desk chair. "I'm sorry, Jay. This had to happen at some point, though I thought you'd have a little more time than this. But after that photo in the paper..."

"What are you talking about?"

"The photo that guy took outside the hospital last month. Right before you took her home to meet your family."

Yeah, right after she'd almost been killed. He'd almost lost her. Had he lost her now? "Level with me. Everything you know. She has to be under some sort of protection, though I thought Matthew was some retired professor type."

Cal slipped the toothpick from his mouth and repositioned it. "He's not?" He tapped some keys on his laptop.

"Not the guy I saw. Maybe a recently retired Navy Seal or Army Ranger, but he can't be over thirty-five and twice my muscle weight." Not that Jay was a wimp. In his department, he was probably the most fit, but couldn't press half of this *Matthew's* likely ability.

"Hmm." His partner hunched over the keyboard for another moment, then backed up and turned the screen toward him. "Meet Samantha Fellows. Father was a police detective in Sacramento... deceased. Mother deceased when

Sammi was a baby."

"Sammi? That's the name the guy said." Jay squinted at an image. The girl was unmistakable. Dani with the tight little smile that she uses when she's about to say something clever. Only this Dani's deep brunette waves were exchanged for kinky, platinum curls resting on her shoulders. And instead of the light make up she usually wore, showing off her natural beauty, this girl was almost clown-like with a spray-on tan, ultra-long black eyelashes, sunken cheeks, and sparkling eyelids. And glossy lips, something between red and brown. "Was Dani undercover or something?" Not such a stretch since her dad was a cop.

"Not so much." His partner turned back to the keyboard, his brow wrinkled. "What guy mentioned her name?"

"Two guys on the hill were looking for someone named Sammi. Arguing about it. That's when she took off through the woods."

"That's not good." He clicked a couple of more keys. "Cap'll have my badge if he knew I was telling you this." He gave a final punch and spun the flat-screen monitor again. "This..." He paused.

The image was of a man. A businessman, but young. Probably thirty-something in a designer gray suit. His dark hair accented striking blue eyes against an even tan. Probably painted on, too. "Okay?"

"Robert Torelli, thirty-two at the time of the photograph. Formerly awaiting trial for the first-degree murder of a policeman... in Sacramento."

Light dawned. "Dani's dad?"

Cal lowered his head. "Sammi's dad."

Gut punched. No wonder she's been so quiet about this around him. She didn't want to put him into the danger that ended in her father's death.

He pushed another button and a new guy joined Robert on the screen. This one bald with a sharp brown beard and bushed eyebrows. He dwarfed Robert with much the same bulk that Jay had noticed in Matthew.

"That's Tony Dimitriadis, Robert's body guard, lackey, and head wrangler."

"Wrangler?" Odd term. "Is the man a rancher?"

"In a tragic sense. Seems to have his thumbprints all over the trafficking links in that part of the country and abroad."

Sick, but hints and effects of human trafficking had been in almost 100 cases over the past few years. "And he killed Dani's... uh, Sammi's dad."

"According to Dani, yes." He fingered the toothpick again and looked away.

Jay gritted his teeth and shut his eyes for a second. Losing his temper wouldn't get him the information he wanted or make him feel any better. Well, punching something—anything—right now would probably make him feel a little better. "Wait a minute. You said 'formerly.' He was up for trial, but not anymore? A technicality?"

"No. An escape." Cal logged off the computer and shut the lid. "Tony D. has been at large for the last couple of months. Sacramento police believe that he helped Torelli get out by bribing a guard in his section."

"And let me guess, one of the guards quit his job." Sounded like a tired police show.

"Nope, just didn't show up. There's a BOLO out on him, Torelli, and Dimitriadis, now. Though they believe that all of them are still in California."

Jay raked his hand through his thick hair. "Not

if the conversation I heard is any indication. And Dani's agent must feel the same way because he picked her up right there on the street."

Cal shook his head and slipped his laptop into a backpack. "I got a feeling you're not going to see her again, my friend."

The punch he'd felt before gave way to a growing, empty feeling that resonated from his gut and ached through his chest. Cal was right. Dani had to be moved for her own safety.

His friend swung his bag over his shoulder. "You need some sleep." He put his hand on Jay's shoulder. "Seriously, dude. There's nothing to be done."

But there was something. Protecting Dani had become someone else's job, but that didn't mean he couldn't help. And before he slept, he'd be sure to have a safety net around her life here that no thug from her past could pierce.

Chapter Two

Three months later.

Dani settled deeper in the chair beside her bed and tried again to focus on the dry text from her Economics class. The topic left her brain foggy and her muscles cramping.

And Matt had the TV turned up too loud. Why couldn't that man turn the thing off when he left the place? But at least he wasn't a messy house-mate. For that matter, his room was so sparse, his biggest mess would be the shavings off his favorite pencil.

She closed her book and switched off her bedside lamp before opening the curtains of her second-floor vantage point. Good, the driveway was still empty of Matt's silver sedan. He'd claimed to have an appointment at the local coffee shop, but it was probably a department briefing with his superiors. Either that, or he was having a fling with the barista. Yeah, right.

Trotting down the stairs, she aimed for the sofa, the only comfortable piece of furniture in the place besides her bed, and the TV remote that teetered on one arm. Time to switch the depressing political news off. She aimed at the flat-screen and froze as a picture of the Dallas skyline showed behind a white, bold-face headline. *Officers Shot in Downtown Dallas.*

A nervous reporter appeared on the screen, taking the remote report. "Yes, Ken, the situation here is far from settled."

A couple and another man who shoved a grocery cart ran past him. The reporter glanced behind him as a shot rang out. "There... as you can hear—"

A policeman rushed into the camera sight. "Get back. What are you doing?" He pushed on the reporter. "Behind the wall. Get down." He pointed at the camera. "Get back, now."

Another shot rang out as the camera jolted and showed the sidewalk for a moment. Someone screamed and the camera came back up at a crazy angle catching the top of the reporter's head. A couple of men grunted and more shots sounded before the scene cut back to the news room.

The audio caught the reporter saying, "He's alive. Get an ambulance in here."

The blonde anchorwoman was caught with her mouth hanging open, but Dani couldn't criticize. Her own was hanging loose.

She bolted to her feet and dashed for the keys that lay atop the table near the front door. If she had to drive the entire three hours to Dallas to be sure Jay was okay, she would. The reflection of the mirror above the table caught her eye. The purple highlights that she'd added to her hair laughed at her. Her short layers, more black than her natural brunette, bounced around her cheekbones.

Robert was still out there, and he still sought her. What good would it do for her to wind up dead? She shoved the thick-rimmed glasses, that her twenty-twenty eyes didn't need, further up her nose and returned to the sofa where she hit her knees beside it. "God, please let Jay be all right. There's no reason for him to be down there. His department is across town. And Friday's are his off-days. He's not there. God, please don't let him be there." She'd prayed prayers of that topic daily, but not so often with panic filling her chest. "Please don't let him be hurt."

If only she could pray that God would bring him back to her. But she didn't deserve him. Had never deserved him. And by now, he knew all there was to know about her. He'd no more want her than he would want a blister on his trigger finger. Though, having her around would be even more dangerous. And painful.

But Matt had been wrong about her heart healing. The pain hadn't ebbed like ripping off a bandage. Instead it grew with his absence. She missed him as much or more, now, than she had when she and Matt first moved out here to Abilene. She scrolled through the news channels for any other information, but only tidbits of what she already knew filtered through. No details and no names.

When Matt came home, she flicked to a movie

station that she'd set up earlier and grabbed her bowl of popcorn.

"Shouldn't you be studying?" He picked up a stray popcorn kernel and tossed it in the kitchen trash.

"I can only take so much of numbers and probability before my mind turns to mush." She'd almost looked forward to returning to school, aside from the business major into which she'd been forced. She crossed her legs at the ankle, trying to display a relaxation that she didn't feel. If only she'd been allowed to take classes in something that interested her like photography or… law enforcement. That would've been a stretch; Sammy Fellows majoring in Criminal Justice.

"Anything I should know about?" He disappeared into the kitchen.

She had to hand it to the man. This ridiculous marriage they pretended had to be as hard for him as it was for her, but he always acted with the same composed demeanor. Detached and professional, if not cold. After all, his life was likely in as much danger as hers now, since he still had to stay connected to Homeland Security and use his real name there. Only a few agents knew about Michael and Candy Davenport and their counterfeit marriage license to complete the ruse.

"I have another essay to write. Don't worry. I won't say a thing about my experience. I'm getting pretty good at making things up." Now that she didn't have to keep lying to Jay and other people she cared about all the time.

"See you in the morning." He ascended the stairs, and a moment later the door to his bedroom, at the front of the house, closed.

She gave him a few moments before clicking back through all of the news stations. Over the course of the next several hours, the only information she could glean was that the shooter or shooters were still at large and that every off-duty cop in Dallas had been called to duty in full search-mode downtown. When she couldn't keep her eyes open, she made sure to switch back to the movie channel before turning the set off and going upstairs to her own bedroom.

Only a few hours later, teetering between fully awake and barely dozing, she cracked open one eye. Light had begun to stream through her curtains. The events of the night before stirred her. She would find out if Jay was all right today, one way or another.

"Cover the other side."

Jay's captain's voice crackled over the personal radio he'd clipped to the armor-coated vest he wore over his uniform shirt. He put his back to the white wall of the small building on the corner of Market and Elm as another short spurt of gunfire rang out, the second he'd heard since he arrived at the makeshift command center set up at Dealey Plaza.

Several voices shouted over the radio. Another officer down. Jay pushed off the wall and trained his AK47, though even with the floodlights, he'd have trouble seeing anyone not wearing reflective gear. Founder's Plaza silently held its breath as Jay glanced around the corner of the small building and pulled back.

Another shot interrupted the peace, but this one had no response over the radio. Looked like the guy wasn't the perfect shot he'd seemed to be. Every other time he shot, one of the officers or the rail security had been hit.

Jay eyed the empty grass between the small building and the college building across the street. No way he'd be able to achieve that site if the shooter was in the building. More than likely, though, the guy had set out as soon as he'd fired. That had been his practice all night long.

Move. The urging came deep within Jay. Without thinking, he dropped to a knee and rolled away from the stone facade. A blast sounded as a bullet ricocheted above his head. Jay did another half roll into the landscaped beds on the other side of the small building. He was up in an instant and dashing straight ahead. The small, log cabin memorial was only a few yards away. With trees and a dark building behind him, his movement shouldn't have been noticed.

Not like it had been against the light stonework of the other building. That had been a stupid choice. He hated being stupid.

Again, a shot sounded, but nothing crashed around him or pinged off the wooden structure in front of him. His radio reverberated with yet another victim. He could see two others congregate over an injured man to his right. One trained his gun toward the RL Thorton building behind them.

"I see him." A voice shouted over the confirmation of aid to the victim. Probably some rookie who didn't realize just how scared he really was.

"Radio Silence." His captain fairly screamed. The last thing they needed was to let the perpetrator know that officers were closing in.

His cool-headed shots were dangerous if not deadly. What would his desperation shots be?

A shadow raced through a parking lot separating the campus from the old county services building.

"On it," Jay whispered under his breath and took up the chase. His heart thundered in his ears and his steps padded against the asphalt. The shadow dashed ahead of him and to his left, skirting the backside of the building, darting between parked cars

Jay accelerated around The Record Grill. The man couldn't get into the empty county building, but the nursing building across the rail tracks were a different story. Lots of windows and glass doors gave entry points and no telling where he might hide. Or what hostages he might find there even at this hour.

Huffing, Jay reached the corner of the building. First glance showed a stationary shadow. He dropped to one knee and rolled as a boom echoed between the buildings. On one knee he paused, pulling back around the corner.

He fingered his radio to put out an alert ping. Better than speaking his location for all and the perp to hear. A drop of sweat trickled down his temple as he did an internal three-count. He whirled, taking aim down the walkway, but the shadow had disappeared. Jay hung back a moment to let his eyes adapt to the dimmer surroundings and scanned the bushes that edged the other building. He leaped over the fence and hurdled the chain dividing the rails from the walkway.

Running footsteps behind him. He halted, flattening into the bushes. Two other officers approached. Jay motioned toward the building front where his most likely entrance would be. He readied his weapon again and turned on the speed toward Record Street.

"Hold it." The shout came from around the corner that Jay sped toward.

"We've got him." A much calmer voice sounded over the radio.

Jay led the others onto the road. The perp was on his knees, hands high. "I'm not armed. I told you that."

Was this the guy? He looked military with dark clothes and boots and an ammo belt strapped across his torso. But he'd given in quick to already be in submission.

An officer, weapon pointed, approached the man.

"You're covered." Jay pointed his AK47 at the figure on the ground.

The other officers added their lights to the spectacle as the nearest man patted down the perp, removed his ammo belt, and cuffed him. "No weapon." Lights flickered across the empty lots on the other side of the street as a line of cruisers stopped against the curb.

"Like I said." The perp had a big mouth for a

guy who'd been firing on police. He was lucky he didn't get his nose busted.

"Where's the gun?" Another cop, a Lieutenant something or other, fisted the shorter man's black tee shirt.

The perp chuckled. The lieutenant showed amazing restraint.

"Here." An officer advanced holding a sniper rifle with his gloved hand.

Jay leaned back against the corner behind him and lowered his gun. His shoulders would take a little longer to lower. He applied the safety on his weapon and lowered his chin, rolling his shoulders forward and back a bit to get the muscles to release. How many people, fellow cops, had this man hurt or killed tonight?

"Sergeant Hunter, so good to see you here."

Jay lifted his gaze to the face of the punk who'd shot at him. Shot at all of them. The man's clean-shaven face showed no sign of sweat, but his eyes, clear blue, pierced Jay.

"Hope to get you in my sights again, soon." He chuckled again as an officer tugged him to his feet.

How did that creep know Jay?

The lieutenant taking charge of the scene turned a scowl in Jay's direction. Probably wondering the same thing.

Marji Laine

Dani left a note for Matt about her trip to the library. She didn't specify that it was the public library and not the one on campus. She stopped on the way at a cafe to get a caffeine fix and hear the latest of the news.

"Good morning, sunshine." The barista who normally waited on her was a terrible flirt and had to be at least a half dozen years younger than she was. "Your regular?"

"Yes. Extra-large this morning."

"Late study night?" He smiled as he took her cash and handed her the change.

"Something like that." She eyed the TV

mounted in the corner of the room. "You think I can borrow the remote for that thing for a few minutes?"

"I don't see why not." He turned to collect it from under a counter. "Just bring it back if folks start coming in. I don't want others to ask, if I can help it."

"Sure thing." She clutched the electronic piece like a gold bar and almost forgot to grab her coffee. After stowing her bag on the cushion of a booth, she started flipping through the channels.

"You hear about the shooting last night?"

She murmured a reply to the guy and settled on a local channel where she'd first heard the story.

The anchorwoman was the same lady as last night, though she wore a different suit in an awful yellow that Dani would have remembered if she'd seen it before. "The Dallas Police have not released the names of those officers who were attacked, but we will bring you that information as soon as it is available. What we do know, to recap, is that a sharpshooter—and the department believes he was acting alone—shot and perhaps killed several detectives and crime-scene specialists as they examined a murder scene in the Historic West End of downtown Dallas last night. The shooter then fired on other police from several vantage points, keeping them at bay for most of the night."

The words *crime-scene specialists* pulsated through Dani's mind. What a terrible scene that would be to clean up. Would Tasha and Tyrone be on the team that had to take that task?

Once again, her roommate Tasha passed through her mind. Dani's abrupt departure pierced her heart. Thankfully, Matt had left word with the East Dallas station captain to let Jay, Tasha, and Ty and his wife know that Dani had left for good.

"More than one off-duty officer endured gunshot wounds as they sought out the suspect, but his movements were calculated, sending off two to three shots in rapid fire, then darting to a new location." The anchor woman's voice took on a sad tone, but Dani focused in on the off-duty officers. Jay? Surely not.

"The shooter's movements through the night almost depicted a chess game, but officers were finally able to surround him near the Southland Life Building. No word yet on the result of the stand-off or on the injured officers."

And no names either, as frustrating as that policy was. Dani ran her thumbnail over her bottom lip. The black paint caught her eye. No one in Dallas would recognize her. Not like this. Not even Tasha. But Matt might split a vein if she disappeared. Still, she could do an out and back and still be home at a reasonable hour. With her decision teetering in that direction, she turned to the TV again as photos of the night before flashed on the screen with *Breaking News* flashing over them.

A new photo appeared and Dani gasped.

"The suspect has been identified as Arno Reynaldi. He has been arrested for multiple counts of deadly assault. Further charges are expected." The screen darkened and went to a commercial, but Dani remained frozen.

Arno. One of Robert's thugs. What had he been doing in Dallas? She shivered and clamped her teeth tight.

Turning her back on the TV, she blew out a long exhale. Then she collected her coffee and thanked the server before pushing back into the sunlight, making for the library down the street on foot.

It had been easier leaving Sacramento. The people she'd been closest to were the ones trying to kill her. But those in Dallas really cared about her, and her heart ached to spend time with them again. Even if it was in the midst of blood and ruin doing a job for the Kellerman Crisis and Trauma Cleaners where she'd been on a team with Tasha and Ty.

For her to come out of hiding, to give herself away would mean these men and women had been injured or even killed for nothing. She couldn't let Robert win. Not now. Not ever.

Still, she had to find out about Jay. She logged into the library computer as a visitor and opened a new j-mail account. Completely anonymous. She typed in a quick note to Tasha without names. *I'm fine, but worried about our mutual friend who serves and protects. In regard to the news, how is he?*

There. With all the emails in the world, that wouldn't hit any meta data searches. She logged off the computer and glanced around. An older man shared the bank of computers, though he was on the other corner. Three or four students had already snagged the chairs down the darkened aisle that faced the wall beside the librarian's desk. Those were the choicest study cubes, but no one sitting there glanced her way.

Even if her note did catch attention, no one would recall her even being there.

Jay's all-night romp through downtown didn't cancel or even abbreviate his day job. He'd barely shut his eyes before his alarm insisted he rise. He needed an energy drink. After his adrenaline dissipated just before dawn, he'd hardly been able to drive the rest of the way home.

Coffee would have to suffice for now.

Cal met him in the cube they shared. "You all right after last night?"

"Confused, but all right." He began to remove his laptop from his pack, then halted. "What's the word?"

"In surgery, serious, critical, but no deaths. Not yet." Cal gnawed on a toothpick.

How? The guy had a hit with almost every

shot. How had he only wounded every time? Jay extracted his computer and snapped it into the charging base that also connected it to the raised, extra-large monitor on the wall.

He sat in his desk chair. Cal was watching him. Obviously, the news about the suspect's greeting for Jay had gotten around. He shrugged. "I don't know."

Cal raised his eyebrows and leaned back in his chair. "Know what?"

The man was brilliant in interrogation, but Jay wasn't supposed to be the subject of such. "I've got work to do." He turned his back on his former partner, former only because of Jay's promotion last spring.

Cal's chair squeaked. "You gonna level with me?"

Now the real questioning began. "Are you going into psychiatry, now. Yes, I heard a shot go right over my head. No, I've never been in a battle like that before. Yes, I thought I might not come home. No, it didn't stop me from moving, but I wasn't the one who caught the guy."

"I knew most of that. And what I didn't, I

assumed, or you'd be an idiot." He paused for a moment. "And?"

"And..." Was it even worth thinking about, let alone speaking out loud? "And, I worried about Dani."

"Dani? Are you outta of your ever-lovin'? That girl is nothing but poison on you."

Jay spun in his chair. "Watch it. I love her."

"Jay has it occurred to you why Arno Reynaldi might have mentioned your name?" Cal leaned over, his elbows on his knees.

"I guess I've dealt with him before, though I didn't recognize him at all."

"No, no priors in this part of the country. Ever. But in California..."

"California?" No way. This guy couldn't be connected to Dani.

"A long list of dubious extra-curriculars in LA and Sacramento." Cal's toothpick wiggled as he clamped on it several times. "Seems the thugs are getting impatient."

A worried crook was a dangerous one. "Dani's in trouble."

"I think you're the one in trouble. Dani's quite

hidden, but you're out there pounding the streets."

He was nothing like a beat cop, but Cal's point was still appropriate. "You think they're trying to get her to surface through me?"

"What other recourse do they have? And after tracking her to y'all's date on Flag Pole Hill three months ago, it's not a stretch that they've learned all they need to know about the two of you. Enough to know you'd be their best chance to draw her out of her hidey hole."

"The shooter wasn't trying to kill cops." His chest hurt. These injuries were on him. His fault. He'd known she had secrets, but he pursued her anyway. Had he not... had he kept his head, those officers wouldn't be in the hospital right now.

"No, I think he expected to be caught and didn't want murder against him. He was only trying to get you."

And what better way to draw all the cops in Dallas together than to start shooting at some of them. His cell phone, still inside his pack started jingling. Tasha's signal.

He clicked to answer. "I'm fine, Tasha." Though *fine* wasn't in the least the way he'd describe what he was feeling at the moment.

"I'm so glad. I was worried. And I wasn't the only one." Her high-pitched voice, like a little fairy's, sang through his phone.

"Give that message to Ty and Carla, too, will you?"

"I will, but I haven't heard from them today. I have heard from a *mutual friend* though. Thought you'd want to know about it."

His spine stiffened. "How, your phone? Is the firewall still installed?"

"Emailed to my computer, and yes, the security is still intact, I think." She didn't sound certain.

"Can you bring your computer to me now?" First, to make sure no one else got Dani's message and then to use the program he'd installed to pinpoint her basic location.

"I'm already en route. Want a coffee?"

The magic word, but checking the computer had priority. "No, thanks. See you in a few." He hung up and glanced at Cal's furrowed eyebrows. "She's made contact."

"That's not good."

Not good at all.

Marji Laine

Chapter Four

Dani pulled into the driveway, but left her Jeep close to the street. She had a class soon anyway and Matt wasn't expected until late evening.

"Where have you been... sweetheart." Matt stood on the porch with his phone in his hand.

Her spine iced. What was he doing here? She glanced over her shoulder at the married-student housing apartments across the street. No wonder he'd called her *sweetheart*. A couple were climbing into their SUV at the edge of their parking lot across the street. Close enough that they'd been able to hear every word.

"Chapel... like always. Required, you know."

She stiffened as he planted a kiss on her temple and slipped his arm around her.

"Good thing you didn't miss Chapel." His casual comment covered this source of conflict between them.

The agency had forced her to take on the façade of becoming a student. If that was her only choice, she insisted on a Christian university since she wasn't allowed to attend church regularly.

Matt had commented more than once that she'd better never miss chapel after making such a stink about it. He pulled away from her as soon as the front door closed.

"You missed your first class." His voice had lowered to it's typical, irritated one.

"I was running late." Well, she was... after driving into downtown to visit the public library.

"I heard you when you left. You should have made it to campus twice." His volume lifted slightly, his arms folded over his broad chest as he stood in front of the doorway to the kitchen.

"I had something I needed to look up at the library." Not a lie. She was so sick of lies.

"And?" He didn't move.

And... what? "I ended up having to go to the library downtown." Again, not a lie. "And I only have an hour for lunch." *So, drop it!*

He still didn't move away from the entrance. "What were you researching?"

Ugh. "Look, I don't have the time to explain the details..." Of what? She could say *of class* but that was a bald-faced lie. Another one.

"All right, let's cut to the chase. I heard your television on most of the night. You have to know about the shooting in Dallas by now."

Heat rose into her cheeks. "You should have been the one to tell me about it. You're the one who can get the information, but no. You refuse to allow me to know anything about the people I've left behind. I didn't even try to talk to you about it because you'll cast my concern off with your typical platitude, *Not my problem.*"

"You need to settle down, right now."

"It is your problem because I care about these people. I left the man I love behind without a word. I'm doing everything you've instructed and trusted you completely in this. You're the expert. The least you could do is calm my fears. But instead you're giving me the third-degree because I had the audacity to try to find out things for myself." Angry or not, she didn't dare tell him about her email to Tasha.

"You can't concern yourself with anything you left behind." His eyes, cold, he glanced past her out the front window.

"Can't you simply pull up the information from last night... the real information... and tell me about Jay? I know you have the ability and connections."

"This isn't my concern--"

"No, of course not. Anything that takes extra effort on your part is out of the question. After all, I'm—how have you always put it—more trouble than all of your other security clients put together?" Forget this. She couldn't sit in the kitchen and calmly eat her sandwich now. She snatched up her keys from the entry table and started for the door.

"You have to put this behind you, Dani."

That wasn't going to happen.

"This is almost over." He caught her elbow. "Nothing has changed. You need to stick to the plan."

She halted and faced him. "A lot has changed. Robert's not in jail, so there's no more October trial date to expect."

"Shhh." He glanced out the window next to the door.

"I've had to leave people, good people, who I care about and who care about me. Have you even contacted them in these last three months to let them know that I'm okay?"

"That's not my—"

"I know, I know. Believe me. I'm fully aware of your *problems* with me being chief among them." She yanked her arm away. "You wouldn't want to hurt one of your fingers lifting them."

"Where are you going?"

"I'm eating out." She tugged the door open and rushed out.

"Okay, sweetheart." Matt followed her onto the narrow concrete porch. "I'll see you tonight."

Sure, *sweetheart*. The thought raged. There was nothing sweet about the man and he didn't have a heart.

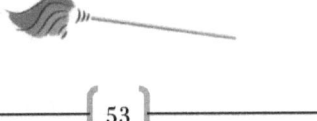

Some defense he was. Jay gripped the steering wheel and guided Cal's white Honda across the wasteland of I-30 on the west side of Ft. Worth. Thankfully, Tasha was willing to look after his dogs for a few days.

"Stop beating yourself up. At least you put the tracking program on Tasha's computer so we could find Dani if we needed to." Cal took a slurp out of a *Gulp* cup. "Though I'm still not sure going all the way out to Abilene is the smartest move to make."

"I don't know what else to do. We have to warn her and her agent that we aren't the only ones to have tracked her communication." It wasn't like he'd have any success making phone calls. Even if he could get connected to the US Marshals, they'd have no reason to listen to him.

Even through his logical argument, the truth emerged. He wanted to see her, had to. "I appreciate you coming with me. I know how you feel about Dani."

"I don't have anything against her personally. She's cute and nice and whatever. But she's not good for you, Jay. You're a straight arrow and she's... well... not."

He couldn't contradict Cal's words in the slightest. She'd lied and kept secrets the entire time he'd known her. "I still think once her past can be put firmly behind her, we might have a future together." How lame he sounded, like a love-sick, whiny, little puppy. "Either way, her agent needs to know of the danger.

They entered the city limits and headed toward the public library, the source of the IP address from the email that Tasha had received.

Once inside, Jay showed his credentials to the lady at the desk. "Can I speak to the head librarian, please."

"She's downstairs." The woman pointed to her left at a stair case that went both up and down.

Jay flicked his gaze to Cal. The man took the silent message and stepped down one of the aisles to do a quick surveillance. Though it had been several hours since the email was sent, people did tend to hang around libraries. Jay headed downstairs. A large bank of computers to his right with a research desk straight ahead.

The woman there hung up a wall-phone as he approached. "I'm Mrs. Widgeforth. You wanted to speak to me?"

Obviously, she'd been forewarned. Jay smiled. "I'm looking for a woman who was here in your library, this morning, about 8:10. Do patrons come in that early?"

"Yes, in fact, we began opening at eight every weekday and have a steady stream until just before nine. What does your... um... person of interest look like?"

"That's what we don't know. She has likely changed her appearance." He glanced at the ceiling above the bank of computers. "I'd like to view the recordings from that camera." He pointed to the glass bulb drooping about three inches from the tiles around it. "Does your computer there have access?"

She began to click at the keys, seeming to enjoy herself. "I think I can pull that up for you. Go ahead and come around."

Cal joined him on the business side of the bar. With barely a glance in Cal's direction, the librarian brought a video onto the screen. The computers were empty. "This is at eight. You can scan through the recording here." She pointed to the arrow keys.

"And, of course, you can print the screen if need be." She pointed to the printer against the wall. "If you need me, I'll be at the other counter." Slipping a *closed* sign onto the counter, she moved away and began helping someone across the aisle.

"Nice lady." Cal smirked. "Warm and friendly."

"She didn't give me any flack for viewing this, so she's got points in my book." Jay fast-forwarded the video until a figure appeared. He paused it.

Cal pointed with his toothpick and stuck it back into his mouth. "That's a guy."

Sure enough, the broad shoulders couldn't have belonged to Dani without a set of football pads. He zoomed through more until a much smaller figure arrived.

"That could be her."

No way. This was a girl, a child almost. Her short black hair had purple highlights that matched her leggings. She wore an overly large, man's dress shirt cinched several times around the middle with a variety of belts and dark black makeup on her eyelids. "That's not Dani."

"Why? It's the right time. Look there. She's

biting her lip." Cal pointed at the screen.

Jay would recognize that mannerism anywhere. "So, she was here." He scanned back over the short segment and selected a couple of images, both front-facing and profile, to print out. "Now what?"

The recording continued to play to the end when the girl, hard to think of her as Dani, hoisted a heavy-looking backpack onto one shoulder and walked out of the camera range.

"You suppose she's a student?"

"Wait." Yes, that's exactly what she was. He scanned backward until the backpack returned to view. A tag flapped on the zipper-pull.

"What is that?" Cal leaned in as Jay zoomed the view, but the tag became a blog of dark colors.

"What colleges are here?"

"Hardin-Simmons is the big one. Also, Abilene Christian University." Cal's clicking on the keypad brought the tag closer and then zoomed out again several times. "Judging from the look of that girl, I'd say she'd stand out at either. They're both Christian colleges."

Could it really have been Dani? If so, what was

she doing in college of all places? "You would think." But then again, looks weren't always typical, especially among students. He'd noticed variations in hair color, like greens and blues, in the youth group at church. More a personality trait than a rebellion nowadays.

"I'm not having any luck here." Cal gave a last thump on the keypad. "I can't even tell if the tag has a picture or letters on it, though I can surmise it isn't a price tag." He waved at the librarian. "Any other views of that bank of computers?" He nodded toward the corner.

"I'm sorry. That's the only view." She approached with a furrow to her brow.

Their many questions could be ticking the lady off. They couldn't afford to irritate her. Not now. Not when they seemed to be so close. Jay's smile wouldn't work, but he applied a casual, pleasant tone. "Do you have other cameras that might have caught her approach or her retreat? Maybe at the front doors or the stairs?"

Her forehead eased and an eager glow lit her eyes. "If she used the elevator, we got a full-faced view of her when she got off." She tapped on the computer in front of Cal. "Here's the feed when we opened this morning."

The closed doors of the elevator filled the screen. Cal sped up the feed, but the doors stayed closed well after forty-five minutes had passed. Dani wouldn't have used the elevator anyway.

"I'm so sorry we couldn't help you." The librarian's heavy, dark brows again ruffled up. Having police asking questions must've been the highlight of her week considering the quiet atmosphere.

"On the contrary." Jay again forced that light-hearted feel to his voice. "We learned quite a lot from this visit. You've been most helpful in our investigation." He maneuvered around the counter following Cal.

She literally clasped her hands under her chin. "Oh, I'm so glad. Let me know if you ever need assistance again."

He waved at the librarian and followed Cal to the automatic, sliding doors.

"Hungry?"

He shrugged. They had to be close. He'd rather keep following the leads until they all petered out.

"I don't know why I even bothered to ask." Cal gave him a light shove in the direction of the passenger side. "I googled a spot that intrigued me. You can eat if you want, or not, but we're gonna stop for a bit."

Maybe Jay could get in touch with the colleges while Cal ate. Maybe the admissions offices. Surely, they were on the brink of finding Dani.

Marji Laine

Dani focused on her driving. The campus speed limit was low, and the campus police did all they could to keep it that way. She rounded the corner near the new stadium and took a right.

People. Interaction. Her extroverted self craved a gathering, even a small one. She headed for Sharkey's. Their burritos were amazing, but the thought of eating anything curled her stomach. Still, it was the most crowded area she could find at the moment.

She could try the student union. But there, she'd likely run into the ECON prof whose class she'd dodged that morning. Bad choice. She drove past the domed building and headed for the shopping center that was a block off campus. Attached to a popular supermarket and coffee shop, Sharkey's always had a plethora of folks inside, but few open parking spaces outside. Luckily, she found one right in front. Though it took some manipulating to get between the truck and the Mini Cooper parked right on the line, she finally backed her Jeep in and prayed Mr. Mini Cooper wouldn't ding her door.

At least being here, she didn't have to think about Matt and their impossible situation. A situation that had no end in sight and probably never would. Robert was brilliant. He probably left the states for someplace golden with no extradition laws the moment he broke out of jail, leaving Dani constantly looking over her shoulder for the rest of her life.

She'd brought that possibility up to Matt more than once, and he let it hang. He didn't have any answers either. And their current circumstances couldn't be any more pleasant for him than they were for her.

Wait a minute, she wasn't about to feel sorry

for Matt.

The image of last night's shooting spree suspect floated across her mind. Arno Reynaldi, one of Robert's more hidden thugs. But Dani had met him once and seen him in the shadows several times over. What was he doing in Dallas? Why was he targeting police? Could his spree have something to do with Robert?

Way too far-fetched. What, so the guy was shooting at Dallas cops because he knew she would hear the news and worry about Jay? She'd have to come out of hiding to make sure he was all right? Ridiculous. Her mind scoffed at the possibility.

However, if Robert knew about Jay—and their relationship hadn't been secret by any means—then what better way to make her surface?

And, in a way, it had worked, hadn't it? Good thing she'd stayed anonymous and only contacted Tasha.

She stepped through the automatic glass door on the grocery side of the building. Should she indulge in some caramel Bugles? A bag teased her from the snack display at the nearest checkout counter. Why not? These snacks might not be the most popular, but obviously someone besides her enjoyed them or they wouldn't still be available. Unless she believed all that stuff about preservatives giving her a lifetime supply in her current grocery store.

After paying for her snack, she considered the line at Sharkey's. No. Not only did her stomach somersault again, she'd be late to her next class. It wouldn't do to have two profs ticked at her. Correction: two profs and Matt.

She turned to the coffee shop line. It was much more doable, and a Caramel Macchiato with an extra shot of espresso sounded like what she needed to get through her Intro to Psych class. Though the chances of her gleaning anything with her mind whirling over last night's events was rather slim.

If Dani was a student, would the admissions offices be willing to relay the information? Especially without a warrant? Jay doubted his chances there. Maybe they should spend some time sitting outside one of the popular student buildings instead of going to lunch in some... where had Cal taken him?

A large grocery store ate up the center of a strip mall across an intersection from one of the colleges. From where he sat, deep in the concrete parking lot, he had no way of knowing which campus. "What is this place?"

Cal tossed his toothpick into the tiny trash bin next to his seat. "This place is a local legend. Best Tex-Mex around. Locals who have moved away make a point to eat here when they visit and ask friends to bring them specials from here any time they come."

Looked like a fast food dive to him. He climbed out of the car. "How would you know all that? Have you been here before?"

"Nah. Shaw, a new kid on patrol, graduated from ACU. When I mentioned we were coming up here, he told me all about this place."

"You told someone we were coming here?" Alarms clanged through Jay's head.

"I didn't tell him why. Only that we were road tripping on a day off. The guy's a cop. Who's he gonna tell?"

The captain? Madison would throw a fit it he knew that Jay was attempting to find Dani. He'd kept her witness protection a secret from Jay for the better part of a year.

Cal held open the door. "You'll get some great food, and you'll feel better about all of this."

"Food isn't going to help us solve this case."

"Yeah, but it might take the edge off your attitude." Cal led him to a counter where a line had begun to form. "And it will definitely take the growl away from my stomach."

Had he been edgy? Probably so. Seriously, what were the chances of him finding Dani in this town? It was larger than he'd expected, but if she was here, she was likely hunkered down in a safe house for the duration of her stay. And with the convict's escape, what were the chances that she would ever be released from her witness-security detail?

They collected baskets of burritos, chips, and salsa and found a seat at the windows that looked out to the filling lot. A motorcyclist roared his engine and walked his machine out of the parking space just outside their window. He mentally checked off the rider. In torn jeans and a muscle shirt, there was little chance that the obvious guy could be Dani, though with his mop of blond hair, he did vaguely resemble her agent, Matt.

"You're supposed to be eating." Cal pointed at Jay's basket while he chewed, then took another large bite of his burrito. "Outstanding." The word squeezed out around his full mouth.

The last thing Jay wanted was food in his already tense gut, but Cal was right. He needed to keep up his energy. He took a bite and let the spices set in. Good burrito. Cal was right about that, too. Movement outside his window caught his eye. A Jeep had parked in the space vacated by the motorcycle, and the driver of the car next to it was trying to wedge herself into her driver's seat. Not an easy task for she was wider than the gap offered by the half-open door. Jay took another bite as the large redhead stomped around her car and got in on the passenger seat.

"Don't look around." Cal's gaze caught his before it dropped back to his basket. He lifted his burrito and talked from behind it. "There's a guy behind you. Not eating. It's why I noticed him. But

I remember him."

Jay leaned over and dipped a chip into a bowl of salsa. "When did you see him before?"

"Just did." Cal nibbled on the burrito. "At the library. Come to think of it, he wasn't doing much of anything there either. Just sort of hanging around."

"Think he's followed us?"

"All the way from Dallas? Nah. I would have noticed." Cal was usually pretty good at pegging tails.

Jay let his gaze drift casually over the crowd. Were there any other followers in there that they needed to be wary of? His search halted at a dark head with a purple-tipped bob, long black shirt, and purple leggings. Dani. She didn't look in his direction, but the profile was obvious: the wide smile with the slight overbite, her button nose and dark, expressive eyes. Even the strange hair and the bug-eyed glasses couldn't hide the face of the woman he loved. "She's here."

Cal had been training a look out the window, probably keeping the guy he'd noticed in his periphery, but he snapped his eyes back to Jay.

"You sure?"

Jay let his chin drop, but kept aware of Dani. "Same as the library video. It's Dani alright, down to the bag of caramel Bugles." But what could he do about it? He couldn't approach her, couldn't even let her see him for fear she'd let her guard down.

Or bolt. And he couldn't let her do that. Not without knowing about her security breach.

"Keep it cool, man. Don't need to give her away at this point." His partner's words only echoed his own concerns.

He hazarded a glance in her direction as she finished paying for her coffee and began to scan the room. "Sit up." Jay brushed his napkin off his lap and reached for it under the table. As he rose, he spotted her turning away, her right hand behind her back clasped around her left arm. The familiar stance pained him.

These last few months had been brutal, wondering where she'd gone and if she had evaded those chasing her. "At least we'll get a license plate." With that they could secure a current address.

She turned when the barista called out a name. What was that? Andy? Sandy? She collected her coffee.

"You need to follow her." Jay kept his gaze on her as she turned toward the grocery store side of the building. A few new people stepped into the coffee line blocking his view.

"Not if I'm going to watch the fellow watching us."

"She'll spot me." He stood anyway. Either he risked her seeing him or losing her all over again.

"Stay casual." Cal handed Jay his car keys. "And bring me my travel cup while you're at it." The words weren't overly loud, but enough to be heard should anyone have been listening.

Jay excused himself through the line of coffee drinkers and the growing line of burrito lovers. Dani exited through the grocery doors. He paused for a moment, then moved to the other side for a better view of where she might be going. She slowed her pace, at the Jeep outside the window where he'd been sitting, and dug in her backpack.

If Jay wanted her license number without letting the guy who'd been following know what he was doing, he'd have to hurry. He darted to Cal's car and grabbed the requested mug, his excuse for being there, then when he reached the space between the grocery doors and the restaurant's windows he put his back to the wall. Dani was already in her Jeep by then, and he made a mental note of her plate as she pulled out. IXG725.

He reentered the grocery doors quickly, but nonchalantly, as though he'd been moving slowly on purpose. "Got it." He held up Cal's travel mug. "Lemme guess you want a full foam, half-caf, double-sleeve, no cup."

"Funny man." He pushed from his seat and picked up his empty basket and Jay's still full one. "Now that I think about it, let's do the Quick Trip across the street. Need gas anyway."

He shuffled to the trash can at a far entrance then ambled back. Jay took a moment to scan the tables, but few stood out. Four men sat alone and all but one of them were facing him. That narrowed their tail down to three guys, but Jay couldn't limit the field further. He fished a couple of bills out of his wallet and dropped them on the table as he passed, retracing his steps toward the grocery store.

"What was that?" Cal's voice was a little loud. Good, he'd caught on.

"A tip. Or did you already take care of that?"

"You don't tip in a place like this. It's a fast food joint. Someone'll steal it right off the table."

"Had my mind elsewhere." He turned and snatched up the bills as a thirty-something, dark-haired guy near the door moved to follow them out.

Bingo.

"You want to hand these to the cashier?" Jay held out the dollars to Cal.

"Save it for next time." Cal chuckled and Jay followed him out, making sure to keep the guy tailing them within sight.

Chapter Six

Dani parked and hiked to the classroom for Intro to Psych. It wasn't so bad, but the business major that had been forced on her required classes she'd never master. Subjects she didn't want to master and had successfully avoided during high school. Now almost thirty, she had to pretend to actually like things like calculus and the stock market. All the while, hiding her true age behind heavy makeup and a rebellious attitude.

How she'd kept up the show for this long was beyond her. Continuing, even for only another couple of months, seemed impossible.

Reaching the lecture hall, she slumped into a

chair at the back and was immediately joined by the blond watchdog that accompanied her to all the classes. The guy looked enough like Matt to be his twin brother, though a much younger version—which was rather the point, since Matt, though buff, couldn't pass for a young twenty-something on his best day.

"You missed first hour."

She pulled out the bag of caramel Bugles and tore it open. "Sure did." This sidekick didn't need her explanation. Matt had already chewed her out for that.

"You want to explain yourself?" He turned a fierce stare on her.

A year ago, she'd have flinched, whimpered. But after being hunted by Robert and a few other murderous factions, she didn't scare so easy. If nothing else, that was a change for the better. She leveled a calm gaze on him. "I've been in class almost two months, and this is my first miss. Consider yourself blessed." She popped a caramel Bugle into her mouth and crunched it.

His eyes narrowed. "Anything else?"

"Nope." She gave him a moment more of her

attention and a half-smile before turning toward the front and pulling out her notebook.

"You made me look bad." The growl in his voice was unmistakable, but he took out an electronic notepad and fiddled with the key board.

"So not my problem." And she wouldn't give it a thought if she skipped another class.

This dude really got on her nerves. Matt's sycophant did everything he could to emulate his idol, and treated Dani with even more disdain than her security lead. The only difference was, despite Matt's impatience and annoyance with her, she had no doubt he would defend her with his life. She wasn't sure this guy would sacrifice a fingernail.

The class wasn't the major yawn she'd expected, but she had to focus again and again on her notes. Continuing to write kept her moderately engaged, and her coffee kept her awake. When her stomach let out a loud growl, she treated herself to a few caramel Bugles, kept out of sight in the depths of her backpack.

Once the professor finished, she packed up her belongings.

"Not so fast." Sidekick Patrick held her upper

arm in a painful grip. "You and I are sticking together all the way back to the house."

She refused to yelp at the pain. "Thanks anyway, but I've got my car."

"Leave it." He gave her a slight yank. Hard enough for her to feel it, but not so much that the people around them noticed. To anyone else, he'd merely taken her arm to lead her out.

Meanwhile, his demand ruined her chances to get back to the library to check for a reply from Tasha. No way she was going to roll over and let that happen.

She waited until even with her Jeep, then flailed her arms out and pushed away from him. "I don't care what her name is." She raised her voice to argument level and gained the interest of several students and faculty standing around. "You don't have any business seeing her after class. Either she goes or I go. But I don't want to even look at you right now." Without waiting for a response, she scampered to the Jeep and hopped in, locking the door behind her.

Patrick seemed stunned for a moment, but recovered quickly enough and bolted after her, as she'd expected. "Candy, open the door."

Nope, no way. She didn't answer as she shoved the Jeep in gear.

He beat the door with his palm. "Let's talk about this." His words sounded reasonable, but pure hatred poured from his eyes.

She pulled away slowly until she had cleared him, then gunned the motor and headed for the library.

"Have we still got the tail?"

Jay turned for a good look at the freeway behind them. The black SUV behind them stuck out like a pimple on the flat landscape. "Got him." But he was so far back, it wouldn't take much for them to lose him. "Are we sure he's following us?"

"He stayed with us all the way out here." Cal was right. The guy had zigzagged behind them all the way through Abilene in a less than direct route to Highway 287.

"So where are we going?" He stared at the GPS on his phone.

"Didn't you say there was a lake out here?" Cal pointed to his right. "Somewhere over there if I'm remembering the map correctly."

"Most of it's dried up if the pictures are current." But there was a small dam with a squarish pool and adjacent cliffs. "There's a turn off about a mile ahead. We'll be dirt tracking."

"Well, if the guy's following, he'll need to catch up when we hit the dirt road so he doesn't miss us meeting our supposed contact." Cal's logic seemed sound, but the rest of his plan sent Jay's alarms to sounding again.

He stretched out his arms as best he could in the tight quarters of Cal's Honda and checked to make sure his weapon was ready. Cal slowed on the highway to get their tail back into view, then took the right turn onto the dry road. Good thing it hadn't rained lately or they'd be window-high in red-dirt goo. As it was, the ruts rocked the car through part of the track.

"Your car isn't going to take too much of this." The sedan wasn't made for such punishment, but the SUV shouldn't have any trouble. Sure enough, Jay spotted the roof of the car over the tops of some mesquite trees that blocked a turn. "We've got him on the hook."

"Perfect." Cal sped up on a straightaway and the dust obliterated the scene behind them.

Jay tracked their location on the GPS. "Hope this baby doesn't go out." Always a risk outside of major cities, but it had held so far. "Coming to a sharp turn ahead."

"Left, or right?" Cal gave him a half-second glance before put his full attention on the road again.

"Left."

This was the one. He shoved his phone under the visor above him. "Wouldn't want to smash that on the first roll." He gripped his gun and disengaged the door lock.

Cal slowed only a fraction as he neared the hairpin. "Watch out for cactus."

Cactus? Jay hadn't thought of that when they crafted their plan. And what a dumb idea. Not only was he jumping blind into what might be a cacti junction, but this was also snake country. Wouldn't do to meet up with a rattler now, even with his gun. But he had no more time to think about it. The area beside the road seemed clear. He opened the door and leaped, letting the force of the turn hurl him past the driven track. He rolled once into the soft sand. Well, that was a blessing. And no rattling around him was a double blessing.

With his ears on high alert for the sound of nearby snakes, or anything else for that matter, he rounded a mass of mesquite trees and ducked behind the squat clumps. As the dust settled, the SUV emerged. The tail had to have some sort of tracking device on Cal's car. He would never have been so far behind them if they were following them by sight alone.

Despite the obvious tracker, the SUV accelerated straight toward Jay. And well it should. If the driver was hoping for Jay and Cal to make contact with Dani, his distance behind them might ruin his opportunity to catch her. But at the rate he was speeding, getting the hulking vehicle to turn at the hairpin would be difficult at best, flattening Jay at worst. But he'd committed to this position. Moving might give their plan away. Already, he could hear the chug of Cal's Honda returning this direction, though he could only see dust being kicked up around the next turn.

The SUV barreled toward him. Jay positioned his gun. Did the driver see him? He almost looked to be aiming right at him. But the large mesquite clump surely hid him well. He kept his focus and waited for the man to turn, giving him a clean shot at the tires. But he didn't turn. He didn't slow. The dust he kicked up looked like a brown tornado bearing down on Jay. He couldn't wait any longer for the man to turn and took aim as best he could.

He pulled the trigger as the driver cut into the hair pin. His left, front tire blew. The car jerked in that direction. With a wave of dirt and dust, it spun out. Jay was up from his crouch and running toward the careening vehicle. It crashed nose first into an outcropping of rocks near Jay. Glass and metal crashed, but Jay lost sight of the driver.

Cal arrived, leaped from his car and took aim through the gap made by his open door. Jay side stepped up to the driver's side of the broken vehicle and took a quick glance inside. The guy was moving slowly, stunned. Jay took the advantage. He opened the door and took aim at the man in one fluid movement. "Hands up."

The guy's groan was his only response, though he didn't seem to have any visible injuries. Cal advanced and Jay slipped his gun behind his waistband at his back. "Up." He shoved the man's hands over his head and reached to unlatch his seatbelt. "You packing?"

With another groan, the guy listed toward Jay and then away from him. Jay patted down his waistband and found a weapon, a Sig Sauer. "Nice." He applied pressure to the man's wrist to steer him out of the trashed vehicle. "Why are you following us?"

"You're crazy." The words were still shaky, but at least it wasn't a groan.

"Where's your tracking device?"

"A tracker. Now that makes sense." Cal came from behind Jay and helped pin the man against the driver's side of the black car, the only windows that survived the crash.

"I'm bird-watching." The man's speech was getting stronger as the stun of the accident wore off. "You cops got nothing on me." He smirked. "Prove that you do."

If only Jay could slap the smirk off his face.

But he had a better revenge. "Who told you we were cops?" It was Jay's turn to smirk. Cal slipped some plastic ties around the man's wrists and pulled them tight. Then he shoved the guy to the ground and bound his ankles.

"Wait. What are you doing?"

"I supposed we could ask you some questions like: who hired you, why are you following us, what did you hope to find. But you wouldn't answer us anyway, would you?" Cal pulled a fresh toothpick from his pocket, unwrapped it, and stuck it between his teeth.

The man pursed his lips together.

"I didn't think so." He tucked the plastic wrapper in his pocket and kicked one of the soles of the tail's shoes. "You should choose your friends more carefully."

"You can't just leave me like this. You're a cop. This is unnecessary roughness." His panic showed in his higher pitch and volume.

"Ha. You're thinking football, scout." Clearly, Cal was enjoying the look of the fear on the man's face as he squirmed.

For whatever reason, Jay had mercy on him.

"We've no jurisdiction here and no protected vehicle in which to transport you." He looped another plastic tie through one edge of the open passenger door, then through the tie on the man's hands. That should hold him for long enough. "There'll be someone along to collect you soon."

During his college years, he'd met the sheriff of Taylor County a few times. Jay's dad attended a statewide conference every year, extending an invite to Jay. Those connections he'd made would come in handy today.

"What happened to your tracking device?" Jay glanced down. The man hadn't dropped it anywhere close.

"Don't know what you're talking about."

"Aaant. Wrong answer." Cal went back to his car.

Jay reached into the SUV, snatched the key fob from the ignition and hurled it toward a ravine in the distance. Then he dug around the driver's seat until he found the man's phone tucked into a pocket in the console. That might come in handy. The only other things in the car were empty fast food bags, napkins, and cups of various styles from a montage of drive-thru restaurants. And glass. Lots of tiny chunks of safety glass. "Guess we're done here."

"No, you can't do this."

Cal returned with a lukewarm bottle of water from his stash in the trunk. "Why? Because you're the bad guy and we're the good guys?" Cal's neck reddened. "You don't live by any standards while ours get higher and higher?"

"Keep it cool." Jay empathized with his partner. Seemed more and more, media reports heralded the ones on the wrong side of the law.

"Is that it?" Cal went on as though Jay hadn't spoken. He grabbed the collar of the guy's black tee shirt in his fist. "We have to follow all the rules of politeness while you can do whatever you darn well please?" He was on his soapbox. Not so surprising after last night.

"That's enough, Cal." Jay put his hand on his friend's shoulder and gave him a tug.

"Yeah, I've had enough." Cal threw the water bottle to the ground near where the man sat and went back to his car.

Jay turned his attention to the tail. "Consider yourself lucky. You could be driving all the way back to Abilene with him."

"You're going to get yours." The man's eyes became slits.

"You better hope not. Right now, you're only suspected of being an accessory to attempted murder and aggravated assault."

"What assault? You're crazy."

Jay held up the man's phone. "We'll talk about how crazy I am after the FBI has gone over your data."

The man paled.

"Yeah, I'm thinking we'll have you connected to the Dallas shootings within the hour." Jay looked at the phone again. "About the time the sheriff's department gets here to pick you up." He nudged the water bottle with the toe of his hiking boot. "Stay hydrated."

Chapter Seven

Dani's short victory over her watchdog ended before she'd traveled a mile toward downtown. The sound of a raucous cry of a bird exploded through her Jeep. Great.

She turned down the volume and ignored the call, then ignored a second one. Matt's voice in her head shouted at her to answer the phone. On the third call, she took a deep breath and answered, clicking it to her speaker. "I didn't miss my class." She applied plenty of cheerleader-smile tone to her voice.

"Patrick called." The hushed growl sounded more dangerous than his raised voice.

"He's a tattle-tail."

"And you're a two-year-old insisting on getting her own way."

Time for some honesty. And a little groveling after she'd lost her temper that morning. "Matt, I know you've got my back, but I can't say the same about Patrick."

Silence met her revelation.

Maybe a little more honesty? "I'm only going back to the public library to check on some research I'm doing."

"The same research from this morning?"

Oh yeah, she'd told him that much. "Do you have information for me?" That would make it easier.

"Come home, and I'll tell you what I know."

This was another ploy to manipulate her into doing things his way. She braced herself and turned into the parking lot at the library. "If you won't tell me now, I'm going to find out for myself."

"Do what I say, Candy. This isn't playtime." His volume went up a fraction.

"No, it's my life. It feels like a chess game with me being the valuable king. I have the power, but I can't do anything, meanwhile the target's only on my back. Not yours or anyone else's. Especially not Patrick's." She shut off the engine.

Again, there was silence for a moment. He was probably motioning something to his precious protege'. "What's the deal with Patrick?"

"Are you trying to stall me, or do you really care?" Likely the first. If she was smart, she'd take off for the computer lab in the basement right now and get her best shot at learning what she came to find out.

"You say you know I've got your back? So why the questions?" He actually sounded sincere.

"Because of all the secrets. If you'd be straight with me, if we could work together like a team."

"But we aren't a team."

"We might as well be, Matt. We're in the same soup now. Your undercover status has been compromised."

"Where did you hear that?" His voice went low.

She'd overheard him on the phone when they first arrived in Abilene, but she wouldn't tell him that.

"When my cover was blown, yours had to go with it. Otherwise, why the elaborate masquerade? My case is the only one you're working now, and you have to have an alias right alongside me."

His sigh carried through the phone. "We'll be there in ten minutes. Don't make me come downstairs for you."

The phone call ended.

Really? He'd just given her permission... well, sort of permission... to complete her search? A giddy smile spread across her face as she leaped from her Jeep. This was her first freedom, and her first victory, since the college decision.

Going through the sliding doors, she smiled at the librarian and trotted down the steps to the computer bank at the base of them. One on the other side was empty and she logged in with her library number. She checked the fake email account. It already had a number of spam contacts, but one email stood out.

Our mutual friend is healthy and traveling at the moment. You get my meaning?

You remember Ty?
Our truck driver for Kellerman's?
Under his calm was a
real go-getting cleaner.
Everything he's done lately
impacts those around him.
Not only Carla, but me as well.
Doesn't seem fair, does it?
Anyway,
nothing here is easy in the
grime biz.
Even last night's clean up was
really hard.

Dani stared at the ceiling for a moment. Tasha's email made no sense at all. She hadn't even signed it.

Digging in her backpack, she pulled out a dollar and hit print on the keyboard before logging out of the email account. She approached the lady at the desk. The woman looked every bit the stereotypical librarian with her dark hair in a tight pile at the top of her head, readers hanging halfway down her nose, and too tight polyester dress hugging her rather large frame. But she had a friendly face, and it lit up when Dani plopped her dollar on the counter. Were they that hard up for money? "I just made a print out."

"Oh, yes. Yes." The woman didn't take her eyes from Dani's face, but took the dollar and fumbled for the change.

Creepy. "Is something... ma'am? Are you all right?"

"Oh, yes. I mean. I've seen you here before." She glanced down into the leather money pouch she'd been opening. "This morning, wasn't it?" The woman slid some coins across the counter.

That wasn't good. Her job was to fade into the background, not be memorable. And the variety of characters currently in the room should confirm that the style of Candy Davenport fit in perfectly with the others who were the age she was trying to fake. Dani looked around. No one looked up or paid her any attention, though the skin at the back of her neck prickled. Especially when she remembered that no one had been at that desk when she'd visited that morning. "I was here, Ma'am, but you weren't." She leaned over the counter. "How did

you know I was here?" She was probably being paranoid, but why the questions?

The woman's face reddened. "I happened to see you on the... security video." Her voice squeaked.

Lead hit the bottom of her stomach. "Has someone been asking about me?" As much as she wanted to hear the word *no*, she wouldn't have believed it.

"Well... I've been a little troubled about that." The woman bit her bottom lip. "I guess I was so excited at being able to take part in a real investigation."

"What investigation?" Dani glanced around the room again. She should never have come back here after sending the first email. She should have checked for the reply somewhere else.

"They said they were police officers, and they seemed so nice and all." Her voice quivered. "But I didn't get their names or see any identification."

"Thank you for letting me know." Inwardly, Dani screamed at the woman. Would this mean she had to move? Again? Maybe she should dig a hole or find a broken-down shack in the mountains.

She snatched her paper from the printer, left her change on the counter and scampered up the stairs. If Matt wasn't here, he would be any moment. And she had a lot of things she needed to tell him.

"Think he'll be all right?" Jay didn't like the idea of abandoning the man, despite his likely connection to a cop attack. At least the day was on the cool side.

"Sheriff's boys should be there within the hour." Cal chuckled. His calm had returned within minutes, per his norm. "And maybe being left out there will give him a chance to get broken before God. Goodness knows he needs to get right."

His partner's attitude about God had done an about-face since the first of the year. And their friendship had grown as well. "No doubt about that." Jay shut his mind against what more the man might be after. Especially if he was working with that Robert guy who was looking for Dani.

Twenty minutes later, Cal pulled into the lot at

the Taylor County Department of Public Safety. "Still got the plates on that Jeep?"

"Yep." Jay tapped his temple and climbed from the Honda.

Once inside, he requested an audience with Sheriff Bell and was greeted warmly by the man. "I'm surprised you remember me."

"Of course." The man smiled a broad smile across his lean, dark face. His ears poked out slightly from curly, gray hair, cut short on the sides and a little longer on the top. "Your dad has been an outright hero to me for years. I was so sorry when he stepped down as sheriff."

Jay introduced his partner and followed the sheriff to a conference table in a room at the back.

"So, what brings y'all to my neighborhood?"

"It's complicated." And in depth. He couldn't share the direct reason they were there without telling the man everything.

"Have a seat." Sheriff Bell motioned to the desk chairs that surrounded the table. "I've got time until your perp gets here."

Jay explained Dani's witness-protection issues and how the Dallas shooting might have a connection there. He also admitted his high-tech adjustments to the email accounts of those Dani was closest to. "One of those accounts, her former roommate's, received communication from Dani that originated here."

Bell nodded. "I shouldn't be impressed, but I am. And the FBI should be worried that someone else did the same thing."

That thought had certainly occurred to Jay. "I put an extra firewall on the accounts, but any hacker worth his salt could break through, and we think someone did."

Cal shifted in his seat. "All this is conjecture, but it's beginning to be confirmed left and right. Originally, we spotted a man at the library, the original location of the email that came in. He was already there when we arrived, standing outside. We saw him again when we stopped for lunch, and he's the one who we detained out at the dried-up lake."

"Following you to get to the woman?" The sheriff's grayed eyebrows furrowed. "How does this connect to the Dallas shooting?"

Jay explained the shooter's connection to

Sacramento, where Dani was from. More importantly, he shared how the man had known Jay's name and recognized him by sight. "As crazy as it seems, we think he was hired to smoke me out in order to put more fear into Dani. Maybe get her to return to Dallas or make the contact they were needing. Which she did."

"I take it, there's something between you two." The older man smiled. "I'm gonna hafta talk to that dad of yours about who he lets hang around his kids."

If Jay had known all about Dani's past before they met, would he still have been interested? Still have fallen in love with her? Jay shoved the questions aside. This wasn't the time to contemplate the matter. And for those questions, there probably wasn't a good time at all.

Cal took up the conversation. "*Something* is right, but we're really here to inform the agents working on her case that her location, if not her identity has been compromised. Like you said, if we could get the connection, someone else could. Apparently did, but he hasn't found Dani. Not that we can tell, anyway."

"But you found her?"

"We haven't made any contact yet." This was taking too long. Sunset was closing in. "We have a license tag that we believe will tell us where she's located."

"Let's take a look." The sheriff rose and led them to a small, cluttered office, closing the door behind them. No wonder he did his conversations in the empty conference room. He tapped on his keypad as he sat in his chair. "Whatcha got?"

"India, X-ray, Golf, seven, two, five." Jay pictured the black and white plate in his mind.

"And we think she's a student at ACU." Cal leaned against the glass of the door. "She had an ACU parking sticker in the back window of her Jeep."

Jay hadn't noticed, but then he was concentrating on the license. Cal would have had a good view of the parking sticker and the girl when she passed him.

"Here's what I have on this." Sheriff Bell angled his flat screen toward them. "The car is listed under Michael Davenport, purchased almost three months ago."

"That would be about right." Jay didn't want to remember how she had left, but the last few months had been more painful than anything he'd experienced.

The older man jotted something on a notepad, tore the sheet off and handed it to Jay. "The address is a house, directly across the street from some of the married housing units for ACU." He tapped a few buttons. "Looks like the insurance includes Michael and Candy Davenport. And..." He glanced up at Jay.

Jay saw the look and bent over to get a better view of the screen. A marriage license?

"One of the things that popped up when I put in the name." The sheriff shrugged. "Not surprising that a girl falls for the man protecting her."

"Thanks for your help." Jay crushed the slip of paper with the address in his fist.

Cal muttered a thanks from behind him. "You know that marriage thing is only a cover, right?" He kept his voice low, his cowboy boots clicking along the linoleum. Jay concentrated on the sound and tried to silence the voice in his head. *She's married. She married that man. That agent. That Matthew.*

The one she always called. Always relied on. All while she kept secrets from me.

Hitting the bright sunlight of the outdoors, he slowed his pace and walked away from Cal's car. What was he doing here? Sure, her agent, that Matthew, needed to know that Dani had made contact and that not only had he been able to pinpoint her location, but someone else had tracked her here. Matt also needed to know that the shooter last night had called him by name. Was likely connected to Robert, and all of that chaos downtown was nothing but a smoke screen to make Dani surface. As ludicrous as it seemed.

But that hadn't been why Jay had come. He yearned to see her again. Desperately needed to hear her tell him that she still loved him. Or that she had only been playing a game and wanted nothing more to do with him—though he'd have trouble believing the latter. But her rejection would help him move on with his life. If, however, she did love him, he was prepared to be erased as she'd been. She'd be better protected with him at her side anyway.

Heat grew in his face. This had been nothing

but a selfish move and one that might end up putting her into more danger. At least they'd been able to neutralize the man sent to find her. To follow them to her. But if they'd never come, he'd never have had someone to follow, or track, or whatever.

For good or for bad, they *were* here. They couldn't leave without making this contact and giving the agent, Mr. Davenport, the information he needed to keep Dani... Candy, his wife... safe.

Marji Laine

Chapter Eight

Robert Torelli had about lost patience with this so-called *elite* team of military-grade trackers. Supposedly, they'd been searching for Sammi since she'd left Sacramento, but not a single hint was to be had until he found his freedom. Then suddenly, they were turning over all sorts of clues.

"What's the word?" He smoothed his dark hair back and straightened his suit coat.

Tony Dimitriadis glanced up at him from where he sat on the sofa in Robert's hotel suite. He spoke into his phone. "Wait a minute." He stood, towering almost a full foot over Robert and easily twice his size, built up with enhancers and hard workouts. "Eddie Alonzo was caught by the two cops he was tailing."

Robert ground his teeth and pressed his lips together.

"But he was able to untie himself and get away before other cops arrived."

Annoying, but still workable. Robert breathed out the pent-up rage.

"Then let's move. I want to be onsite before sunset." He snatched up his gun case. Sammi Fellows was his to take down. Leaving him was bad enough. Nobody left him without deep regret. But turning him over to the cops... for this she would die at his own hand. He couldn't move to his new Caribbean home until she was done.

Tony made a call to the pilot as they moved down the hallway. "Pilot's ready. What's the plan?"

"Is Eddie still in the wake of that police sergeant and his crime scene partner?" Even though Robert knew the name of Sammi's most recent lover, he had no desire to speak it out loud, especially when the man was simply a piece of soon-to-be collateral damage.

"He's way behind them, but the satellite feed is working well enough." Tony pocketed his phone and rubbed his hand over his shiny head. "And get this. The cops took his phone. Still have it probably."

"How was he able to reach you?" Was this a set up?

"He gave a sob story to some old guy who lived nearby. Borrowed his phone." Tony snorted. "Borrowed his truck, too, from the sound of it."

Good. "They are still in Abilene?"

"Yes, sir, Mr. Torelli." Tony stepped into the elevator and pushed the button as Robert entered. He went to the back and took hold of the stabilizing bar. Why did they have to make these glorified packing crates so small. The descent was rapid. Too rapid and the box careened to the right. Perhaps not careened, but there was indeed a slight shake to the floor. Robert wiped at his forehead and tightened his grip on the bar.

Tony hadn't stopped talking during their trip down the Dallas tower, though what he had said would remain a mystery. Robert composed himself during the final few seconds before the doors opened, holding his breath. Then he stepped into the lobby with his normal air of control. Nothing could break him. He always chose the highest buildings for his hotel stays and forced himself to sit by the windows or stand on the balcony. And the elevators, they were merely the culmination of his irrational fears. "We'll take the plane to the Abilene airport. I suppose they do have an airport?"

"Yes, sir. No terminals, but all we really need is a runway, right?"

Robert didn't respond to him. "Have your tracker stay on the two police. And you should call him." He caught Tony's eye. "On his appropriated phone."

"Anything in particular you want me to say to... *him*?" He reached the limo first and held the door open for Robert. Then he climbed in on the other side.

Robert contemplated possible messages to the policemen. "They don't realize the sand has almost emptied from their hour glasses. Make sure they have no fears about such things. We wouldn't want them to experience undo worry."

She's married.

In his world, that meant taken for good. Permanently off his radar. Not because his mom or dad or church spouted some rule, but because the Bible spoke marriage between one woman and one man as the ideal. And because the Spirit living inside him confirmed that necessity no matter what his heart wanted.

He kicked a piece of broken concrete at the edge of the DPS parking lot and stared at the fenced-in field next to him. A lone longhorn bull tugged at scrub grass. It's brown and white side stood out in the graying weeds of Indian summer.

"Pull it together, Jay." Cal slid a pair of aviator sunglasses out of his shirt pocket and slipped them over his eyes. "We've got a job to finish."

Jay nodded. He wasn't gonna be over this news anytime soon, but he followed Cal back to the Honda. The poor car was covered with red dirt like it had been through a dust storm.

Cal got in behind the steering wheel and punched in something on his phone, likely the address for guidance. Then he hesitated with his hand on the key. "You knew this relationship wouldn't work."

"I thought it could. I knew she had secrets and wanted to keep her past from me. I suspected the protection, though not to this extent."

Turning the ignition, Cal stayed silent. He backed out of their space and merged into the light side of traffic. "You know as well as I do that most people in protection aren't innocent themselves. They're there because they made a bargain, to achieve their so-called freedom for ratting out their buddies."

"That's not always true." He knew innocent victims who'd had to go under simply for being in the wrong place at the wrong time.

"Not always, no. But in Dani's case..."

Jay turned fully to the man in the driver's seat. "What are you not telling me?"

Cal shot him a look. "Don't make me wreck this car. It's almost paid off."

"Alright." Jay crossed his arms in front of him, like a stranglehold on his emotions. "I'm calm."

"This marriage of Dani's, chances are it isn't

real."

"She's living with the guy." He halted his thinking there, wishing there was a way to disconnect this Candy Davenport from the woman he loved.

"Well, she's done that before."

Jay's gaze went back to Cal's face, and he fisted his hands to keep them in place. "What are you talking about?"

"In Sacramento." Cal glanced at him again. He shook his head. "She wasn't married, but she was engaged and living with Robert Torelli."

"You're making that up." His voice had become a growl and the car, the street, everything around him disappeared as he saw Dani's face. Her sweet smile when she spoke about her faith. The sad lilt to her voice the time she mentioned her father. "You're not talking about Dani."

"Right. I'm giving you the facts on Sammi Fellows, formerly of Sacramento, California." To his credit, Cal didn't take out a toothpick and gnaw on it like they were discussing last night's Texas Ranger game. But his casual voice grated on Jay's nerves. "She'd been living with him on his estate on the edge of Folsom Lake for almost a year before her dad was killed."

The news heaved itself onto Jay's gut, crushing any remains of... what? Hope? Yeah, nothing left there. He leaned back in his seat. "Let's just get through this and get back home."

The sound of a generic ring-tone startled him. It sure wasn't his, and Cal's phone had nothing but hard rock on it.

"Check next to your seat." Cal pointed to the crack between the console and Jay.

He shoved his hand into the depths. His fingers touched metal. Vibrating metal. He retrieved the phone. This was the one that Jay had taken from their tail's SUV.

"Lemme." Cal took it from him and hit the receive button. "Yo." He raised his tone a bit, very un-Cal-like.

He pulled into a strip mall parking lot. The voice on the other end of the call talked away. The words were lost, but the voice had the lower tone of a man. Was this the one who hired the tail?

"Yeah." Cal continued to impersonate the tail and did a pretty good job of imitating his voice.

"I'm still on them."

He listened again for a few seconds, then. "Toward Brownwood." About eighty miles southeast of Abilene, that would lead any thugs to a dead end.

"Sure." Cal hung up.

"Nice job. You could be our friendly tail's brother."

"I got a knack for voices. What can I say?" Cal pulled back onto the main road and paused while the GPS lady gave her status and next direction. "Okay, so the guy didn't give his name, but I got the feeling it might have been this Dimitriadis dude."

"Did he say anything about Da... uh... Sammi?" Not using her name wouldn't ease the pain, but maybe he could disassociate himself with her better.

"Not in so many words, but he did say to stay on the two cops. They had a line on the girl."

"So, whoever is behind this doesn't have the *line on the girl*, is that it?"

"That's the way I read it." Cal pulled a toothpick from his shirt pocket. "The guy also said that the trouble I'd been having with my tracking device was only going to get worse. Something about a blip in the unit. That I couldn't depend on it anymore and to keep the cops in sight at all times."

"I knew he had to have a device on this car." Though searching all nooks and crannies would have been impossible outside of high school shop class. "Good to know it isn't working."

"Not like our guy could be following us anymore anyway."

True. "But with it glitching, nobody else can pick us up."

"Yeah, that's good news."

Of course, the best news was that whoever hired the tail thought he was still on the job.

Chapter Nine

As Dani emerged from the library, Matt was steering his silver Camry into the empty space in front of her. Patrick, in the passenger seat glared at her. She kept her mouth closed, having already made both men angry today.

Matt climbed from the driver's side without looking back at his passenger. Good thing. Patrick's glower practically melted the windshield.

"Keys." Matt held up his hand, and Dani tossed them to him. He handed them off to Patrick who exited the vehicle.

"I can drive myself home." Not that she had anything to hide, but she hated the thought of that man even touching her steering wheel.

"Get in." Matt climbed back behind the wheel.

Dani did as she was told, watching Patrick make his way down the row to where her black Jeep rested under a tree. She shoved her backpack to the floor.

"You find out what you were looking for?"

She took a breath. He didn't seem mad. "I've learned that Jay wasn't hurt during the shooting." She thought about the rest of the note. It still made no sense. "That's about all."

"So, what do you have against Patrick?" His question was conversational, more words than she usually got out of him unless he was in a rant. But there seemed to be something lying underneath his question. He zigzagged around a car stopped in the center lane.

She shook her head. "A feeling, only. This is all just a job for him."

"It *is* a job." He slowed to a crawl behind an eighteen-wheeler turning onto the road.

"I know that." She rolled her gaze to the ceiling. "But you actually care about what you're doing. At least you seem to."

Matt turned his head briefly with a sidelong look. But the increasing traffic commanded his attention.

She shifted in her seat to look at him. "I know I irritate you worse than all your other clients put together, but I trust you, Matt. I rarely like what you tell me, but I know you want me to survive this. If only to put Robert behind bars. I can't say the same about Patrick. I think he's only in this to impress you and fuel his ambition for a higher ranking and more respect."

He glanced at her again, still creeping behind the knotted traffic, then looked back at the road and rolled forward a few feet. "I say that to all my clients." His voice barely above a whisper.

Stifling a smile, she looked out her side window at a harried UPS driver who slammed his palm against his steering wheel. "I figured as much."

Silence filled the car as traffic began to move until he reached a red light. He turned to look at her. "I do want you to survive, Dani. And not only to put Robert Torelli in jail. You're like the pesky little sister I never wanted." He gave her a half-grin, reached over and ruffled her hair.

Not exactly a glowing compliment, but they seemed to have reached an understanding. Maybe he would treat her more like a team member instead of a child, but she wouldn't hold her breath over it.

"I emailed to Tasha at the library."

"Yeah, I figured you emailed someone. At least you didn't make the connection from the campus library or your home computer."

"And I did think to make an anonymous account with bogus information." Maybe she should have told him all of this earlier. "I also didn't name names."

The light turned green and he crossed to the next intersection, stopping again. "I didn't have the information. If I had, I would have told you."

She pulled out the printout from her email. "Well, Tasha sent back a strange note." She held it up for him to see. "Most of it's about Ty being a great worker, but she wrote it almost like a poem with the way she did her line breaks."

He glanced at the paper, but the light turned green. He made his turn only to get caught again with merging traffic due to unexpected construction. "Let me see that."

She spread it out and hit the dash light so he had the best view. She didn't need to read it again, but suddenly letters jumped out at her. "Oh, my gosh."

"What is it?" The traffic picked up. Another light, this one green, lay ahead and then they would be clear of downtown.

"It's an anagram."

He got caught at the light and turned toward her.

She tracked her finger down the page. "'You... rein... dan...' No, that's 'You're in—'"

"Down." Matt shoved her face into the console.

Her lip pained her and blood filled her mouth. Matt stomped on the gas, and the Jeep darted into the intersection as glass crashed and showered her with little prickles. The car jerked left and right at a building speed. Car horns honked. Wheels squealed. Dani clung to the console with both hands. "Slow down, Matt."

But he continued to accelerate.

She hazarded a glance upward. Matt's temple

had a deep gash. Trails of blood tracked down his face and into the collar of his denim shirt. "You're bleeding."

"Stay down and hang on." The car jerked to the left. The force shoved her against her door for a moment. Some of the glass dug into her thigh as she slid over it. She pushed against the door with her forearm and felt another sharp sting.

"Is someone following us?" Why else would he shove her head down?

She felt the car coast for the first time.

"No." He made a gentle curve and the car slowed even more. They had to be close to the safe house. "There was a delivery van parked at the curb."

A delivery van? "And they happened to break my window?" What had they been delivering?

"No *happened* to it. The man wore a ski mask." Matt huffed out the words and took another turn. "When I stop, you wait until I get to you before getting out. Then run to the side door and let yourself in. You got that?" His voice betrayed pain.

"Are you okay?"

"Do you understand?" His voice became a

shout.

"Yes." She equaled his volume and dug into her bag for the house key. Fisting it, she waited while Matt pulled a little too sharply into the driveway. The back end fish-tailed when it left the concrete and hit the gravel. The corner of the console caught Dani on her left cheekbone. That was going to bruise.

The car came to an abrupt halt. Matt leapt from his side. Her feet crunching quickly through the rocks as he jogged to hers. He stood in front of her door with his hand tucked under his shirt at his back. Likely clutching the gun that he hid there. She scampered out and sprinted for the kitchen door with her key at the ready. Pushing through, she went straight to the bathroom and reached into the lower cabinet for the first aid kit.

"You all right?" Matt's voice echoed against the linoleum in the kitchen.

"Fine." She returned and found him sitting at the kitchen table, his forehead on his fists. "Here, let me see."

"I'm okay."

"You're bleeding." She nudged at his hand,

and he straightened.

"That note. The anagram." The blood had dripped into his eye, and he blinked and rubbed at it.

"Let me." She put a gauze pad against the wound at his temple. "Hold that there." She guided his hand to the pad. "Press against it to stop the bleeding."

"What did it say?"

He wasn't going to drop this. That was brutally clear.

Head wounds were always messy. And though she had no trouble cleaning up after the deceased, she didn't much like cleaning the wounds of the living. She dabbed another gauze pad at the corner of his eye. "Did the glass hit you?"

He sighed. "I don't think so." He shut his eyes tight, then blinked several times. "You going to level with me?"

She moved to give her hands a thorough washing. "It said, 'You're in danger.' I don't know how Tasha would know that unless, maybe she spoke to Jay."

His exhale sounded like a growl, and he

slumped lower in the seat. "I'm not sure he even knows anything. His captain kept all our conversations private, though Jay's partner was in on one of them."

She knew all of that. She'd been there for the interviews. "I need to check on this." She glanced under the bandage. The bleeding had slowed. "This looks bad. If you weren't hit by the glass, how did you get cut?"

"Shot."

The single word boomed through her head with genuine pain. "What?" There hadn't been a gunshot. No sound but the glass breaking. "I didn't hear--"

"Silencer."

"Matt, I'm so sorry." She was going to get him killed before this was all over.

"No need to be." He glanced up and locked eyes with her. "He wasn't shooting at you."

Marji Laine

Chapter Ten

"This is the address."

Jay looked up at the red brick house as Cal made the announcement. Directly across from some of the campus dorms, this place probably had plenty of security drive-bys, though the buildings were surprisingly windowless. Only the edges of a few patio doors could be viewed from the road. And with houses on only two sides, there weren't many nosy neighbors. "Black Tahoe at the curb. Silver Camry in the driveway. No Jeep."

"Maybe she's still in class." Cal continued his slow progress down the well-lit street, then turned around in one of the dorm parking lots. "You ready for this, kid?"

Not exactly. "Of course. The agent needs to know that there was contact, and that we aren't the only ones who followed that trail here." Once they passed that information along, he'd wish her God's protection and blessing and say goodbye.

"Let's pray over this, then."

Those words coming from Cal still made Jay smile even though he heard them fairly regularly nowadays.

"God, we're trying to do the best we can, right now. Trying to help someone who needs it." Cal talked to God the same way he talked to Jay. "I guess You know all about that. And You know the problem. All the emotions involved. Please don't let Jay be hurt any more than he already is. Please keep Dani safe for Your sake. And please put those murdering... those evil men, who exploited Your precious little ones, into jail."

"Amen."

Cal pulled back into the street and brought the car to a rest alongside the curb in front of the house.

Jay unfolded himself from the seat and stepped into the browning grass of a wide and clear yard.

They were probably already under surveillance. "Windows on all sides."

"I noticed that."

Jay did a slow turn as he advanced on the house. No other cars on the quiet street. No loud coeds at the dorms. Though lights peaked out from some of the patios, there was no other sign of life. He faced forward. "I should do this."

Cal hesitated. "You sure?"

Jay glanced at him. "Yeah. I need to do this."

His friend nodded. "I'll hang back here, then."

"Keep an eye on the street." The last thing they needed was another tracker, though those chances were slim since according to the call, the tech was no longer working.

Jay stepped up three concrete stairs and rang the doorbell, eyeing the viewer that was in the center of the door and about chin-high. Who might be on the other side of that? He shifted his weight to his left. The house wasn't that big. Someone could have come down from the attic by this point. He rang again and followed it with three hard, knuckle raps against the door. Hmm. That wasn't wood. It was metal. Maybe an aluminum insulated door? Still no sound. He leaned over the door with the intention of pounding this time, but halted.

Something cold pushed against his neck, under his right ear.

"Easy there, friend." A figure in the shadows patted the small of his back. "Carrying surprises, I see."

Jay held his hands high, trying to place the voice. It wasn't the man who had been tailing them was it? Had he led the guy right to Dani?

"Easy yourself, there, *friend*." Cal's voice he recognized. His partner stood in the bushes opposite the figure beside Jay. "You okay, kid?"

"Feeling stupid." Jay took both guns from the man's raised hands. He tucked his into his waistband again.

Cal nudged the man into the light. The same blond who had driven Dani away. Closer inspection aged him at mid-thirties or maybe early forties, despite his weightlifter appearance.

Jay swallowed his frustration and held out his hand. "It's about time we met, don't you think?"

The man scowled and ignored his hand. "Inside." He walked them around to the side entrance, and they stepped into an old-fashioned kitchen all in black and white like a 1950's television show. "Mind telling me what you're doing here?" He closed and bolted the door behind Cal.

"Calvin Cutter, I don't think we've met." Cal put his hand out, but the man ignored him as well and moved to the refrigerator.

"I've met you, Cal. On the phone anyway. Matthew Donaldson. I was Dani's contact for witness protection." He pulled out a bottle of water and offered them one.

Jay waved away the invitation. "Was? I saw you drive her away back in Dallas."

"What, two... three months ago? You think I'm still working on that case for this long?" He took a swig from his bottle and turned toward him. A neat white bandage covered his temple. "That girl's a pain in the neck."

"We know she's here, Matthew." Jay took a step forward and laid Matthew's gun on the kitchen table. "Unless something happened to her when you got that." He pointed at the bandage.

Matthew wiped the back of his hand across his

mouth and retrieved his gun. "You might have just signed her death certificate."

"She's already in danger." Cal leaned over on the back of a vinyl-covered chair. "That's why we're here. You need to know what's going on."

Tucking his gun behind his back, Matthew's eyes flicked from Jay to Cal and back, scrutinizing Jay's stare as though he could see through to his very soul. Finally, he dropped his gaze and shook his head as he moved through the living room. He tapped on a door under the stairwell three times and then once. It cracked open.

"Oh, good. I was worried." Dani's voice. The door opened wider. "How is your head?"

Then Jay caught her gaze and her eyes opened wide. "Jay?" She threw herself into his arms almost knocking him over.

So much for playing it cool.

He wrapped his arms around her and breathed in her essence, throwing aside what he'd learned about her past and her current situation.

"I've missed you so much. I was so worried when I heard what happened in Dallas."

Her whispers in his ear jerked him back to

reality. He forced himself to release her and pulled her arms away. "The attack in Dallas is why we're here."

"But you're all right, aren't you?" She stepped toward him again.

He turned away and faced Matthew Donaldson. "I was there when they arrested the shooter."

Matthew moved toward the kitchen table and sat. "Obviously, I should be interested in this."

Cal pulled out a chair and joined him. "The shooter was from Sacramento. Arno Reynaldi. Had you heard?"

Matthew shook his head. "Of the shootings? Of course. But I haven't gotten any word yet from my offices if that's what you're asking."

"I'm asking about Arno Reynaldi. He has quite a long list of indiscretions in California." Cal leaned forward, but Matthew didn't seem interested.

"He worked for Robert Torelli." Dani spoke up from behind Jay. He moved aside as she stepped forward.

Matthew straightened. "Why don't I know his

name?"

"He went to jail before... everything... I guess he's been released." Dani slipped the glasses off her face and laid them on the kitchen counter.

Jay put his hand on the back of one of the empty chairs. "When he was arrested, he recognized me by sight. Called me by name."

"You've dealt with him before?" Matthew's face was animated, despite the bandage and the weariness his eyes had shown a few moments before.

"Never."

Cal chimed in. "As far as we can assess, he's never been to Dallas. At least, his name has never come up."

Matthew squinted. "So, you're saying the downtown Dallas shooter... that all that... had to do with...." He pointed at Dani. "That's a little overkill, don't you think?"

Jay's cellphone rang out and he checked the screen. "It's Sheriff Bell." He held the phone out to Cal, then turned back to Matthew. "From what I've learned about Robert Torelli and the business he's in, it seems to fit his MO. Manipulation.

Terrorization. And always control."

"This is Cutter." Cal answered as he walked through the door to the room they'd left a few minutes before.

Matthew groaned slightly as he stood. "If you're right..."

"That's not all." Jay put his hand out. The man might as well stay seated for this. "I set up security around our accounts. Mine, Tyrone and Carla Reid's, and Tasha Sanderson's, Dani's former roommate."

"That's how you tracked us here." Matthew looked at the ceiling, the muscle in his jaw churning.

"Yes, and I also found a breach in the security. When Dani emailed Tasha, we weren't the only ones who noticed it. In fact, there was already someone watching the Abilene Library when we arrived."

"And you led him here?" Matthew jumped to his feet, fire in his eyes. "Of all the—"

"No. We let him chase us toward Brownwood then got the drop on him. By now, he's cooling his heels in the Taylor County lock up with a friend of mine, Sheriff Sam Bell."

Cal came back into the kitchen, his cheeks, normally a little on the ruddy side, were more beet-like than usual. "We need to leave. Now."

Matthew grabbed keys from the counter by the sink and pulled his phone from his back pocket.

"What's happened?" Dani moved closer.

Jay slipped his arm around her, like the appendage had a mind of its own.

Cal scowled at him. "The guy we grabbed. Sheriff said his men combed the entire area. Found the SUV, in flames. No sign of the guy at all."

Dani shut out the chaos that surrounded her for only a moment and drank in the joy from being in Jay's arms one more time. *Thank You, thank You, Lord.*

"Get your backpack." Matt woke her from the reverie with a shouted order. The poor guy looked half-awake anyway. The last thing he needed was her to delay their departure. She trotted into the safe room under the stairs and retrieved the pack.

What he needed was a hospital, but he wouldn't consider that. Especially not now. He was talking into his phone, probably to Patrick.

A car's headlights tracked across the wall from

a gap in the curtains. Jay pulled his gun from under his blue button-down. Cal peaked through the blinds. "Black Jeep."

"That's mine." Dani wondered why Patrick had taken so long to bring it back.

Cal continued as though she hadn't spoken. "One guy, blondish, in jeans and a tee shirt."

"He's with me." Matt jogged up the stairs.

Cal let the guy in when he tapped on the front door. "What the..." He went for his weapon, but Jay raised his own as Cal closed the door.

"We're friends." Jay kept his gun trained as Cal removed a weapon from under Patrick's shirt.

"You don't look like friends." He glanced at Dani. "Where's Matthew? If something's happened to him, I'm the one in charge not some glorified office boys with shields."

Jay, lifted the nozzle of his gun then slipped it back into place behind his back. "We were only delivering a message. But it seems you might need our help."

"I don't need anybody." Patrick scowled in her direction. "We're leaving, Mrs. Davenport."

"Not with you, I'm not." Why would he think

something had happened to Matt anyway?

"Second floor is swept." Matt came barreling down the steps carrying a loaded laundry basket. "I've spoken to Dwight." He looked at Patrick, who had paled a bit. "He's still upset about what happened the last time you used his place, but he's willing to give us the key anyway."

"That might not be the best answer right now." Patrick's volume grew from a virtual whisper to an insistent declaration. "If we're compromised here, we should take her somewhere else."

"No time." Matt shoved the basket at Jay and handed him his car key. "Put this in the back seat of the silver sedan in the driveway."

Jay went out the side door. Dani stiffened.

Cal followed him. "I got your six."

Good. Someone needed to keep an eye on his back.

"You." Matt pointed to Patrick. "Go to Dwight's office and ask for Henry. They'll give you the key to the safe house, and two other agents are coming with you. Get the place unlocked and we'll be there in an hour."

"I still think we should head east." Patrick

paced across the front room and turned back. "Drive to Georgia or somewhere up the coast. They'll have no way of finding us." She'd never heard Patrick actually argue with Matt before. Usually the man was a puppy, enthusiastic about showing off for the master.

"They found us in Dallas, found us here in the west Texas dirt. Going a different direction, even to Mexico, is a waste of time." Matt straightened and looked at Dani. "Robert's here."

A chill oozed down her spine.

"He's not going to rest until he finds you. And while he's close, we need to find him."

"Don't you think that's taking a big risk?" Patrick paled again.

Matt looked at him, then back at her. "What do you think?"

She breathed in. He was asking her? "There was a reason to hide while Robert was in jail. I couldn't testify if I was dead. But with him running free, targeting me, I have no one to testify against." She swallowed. "If he's here. We need to go on the offense. The defensive tactic has only been minimally successful."

"Agreed." He pulled out his phone and dialed but pointed in Patrick's direction. "Get the key." Despite his injury and its effects, he was in full control. "We'll be at Dwight's house in an hour."

Patrick positively growled but was heading toward the front door as Cal and Jay returned to the kitchen.

"Hey, wait." Cal pulled out Patrick's gun and handed it to him. "Think you might need this."

Patrick only scowled then jogged out the door.

"You're welcome." Cal raised his volume and gave him a wave as he shut the door and bolted it. He put down the shades. "Might as well make it hard on those coming to see inside."

"Good thinking." Matt gave him a half-smile. "You ever thought of working for the US Marshals' Office?" He started packing up his computer bag.

Cal chuckled and peaked through the blinds in the front room. "Nah, I like donuts too much."

Jay closed in on her and lifted her backpack onto his own shoulder. "You okay?"

"Now that you're here, I'm better." While she spoke the truth, concern tied her in a knot at the same time. "But you need to go back home now."

The muscle in Jay's jaw tensed. "Dani, I'm a cop. I'm more used to danger than you are. And I'm not going to let the... let you put yourself in the line of fire without being there to back you up."

"You're not a cop here. And this isn't your job." He had to leave. The chances of any of them surviving this were a coin flip. Jay didn't need to be involved.

"I came here to warn you."

"And you have. Check. Job's done. Take Cal and go home."

"You ready to go back to Dallas, Cal?" He raised his voice, but didn't take his eyes off her face.

"And miss all the fun? Heck no! I'm hoping to come face to face with our little tail again." Cal laughed and kept his face close to the blinds.

Fine. Looked like she didn't have a choice. "Number one rule applies."

"And what's that?" He brought his face close. His aftershave brought back enough memories and impressions to whirl her into a tizzy.

She blinked twice to regain her composure. "Don't die."

A tight smiled crossed his face. "I'll do my best." He tapped her nose with the end of his index finger. "Goes both ways."

"We ready?" Matt's bellow indicated he'd finished his packing.

She slung the pack over one shoulder and the first aid kit over her other. "Ready."

A generic ringtone commanded the attention of everyone.

I should have known she was nothing but trouble.

Robert Torelli descended a few steps to the tarmac of the runway in Abilene, a mere weed in the West Texas dirt. He adjusted his holster under his jacket. Coming out here had been his own idea. He should have simply put a higher price on Sammi's head, but he wanted to have the pleasure himself. Wanted to see the fear choke the laughter out of her gentle brown eyes. Wanted to kiss her lips one last time. Before he blasted a bullet into that troublesome conscience of hers.

He could enjoy his freedom only after he exterminated her.

"Car's here, Mr. Torelli." Tony ushered him to the door of the plane and followed him down a short set of steep stairs. "I heard from Eddie Alonzo again. He'll meet us here soon, coming in from the south."

Robert climbed into one side of the limo and waited for Tony to get in on the other. "And Alonzo still has the policemen on his radar?"

"Yes, sir. Says they're on the north side of town, but the data gets clearer as he gets closer."

It wouldn't be much longer. Almost a year had passed. He could imagine the surprise that would light Sammi's eyes. Such a shame that she'd exchanged her beautiful white-blond curls for the drab brown hair that he'd seen in the news photo. She'd gone to waste without him. She must feel it. Having to live in a tiny apartment, sharing everything with a virtual stranger. Not to mention the cop that was keeping her company. Like a person of that measly occupation could treat her to the luxuries Robert had lavished on her. How she must have cursed her choices. And she would again, when he caught up with her. She'd beg him to take her back.

And maybe he should. Maybe she'd do better rotting as a lot lizard in some town near the Mojave. She was still young enough to add a couple thousand a night to his enterprise. "Make a call."

"Sir?"

"I want to make sure the policemen, watching over my sweet Samantha, have all their fears put to rest. We want the full element of surprise on our side."

"Yes, sir."

Robert checked his Rolex. This would be a night he'd remember for a long time.

Chapter Eleven

Cal held up one hand and pulled the tail's phone from his jean pocket. "Yo." He used the higher pitch again, but it didn't sound quite as spot on as it had the last time.

"Amarillo," he said after a few seconds of listening. "A hotel."

Jay wondered at the questions. Were they trying to keep him on the line?

"Looks like." Cal lifted his chin in Jay's direction.

He took his partner's place at the windows, but the street was as quiet as before.

"Will do." Cal hung up. "Same as before. I

(their tail) have to stay on the cops (us) because they (we) have the only lead. The tech is bad, so none of the planted tracking devices work."

Jay kept his eyes on the street. "But we know the tail got away. Likely went back to them."

Matthew went to the side door and looked out. "So, what they said is all lies and they probably know we know that. Hunter, keys."

"On the counter." Jay moved away from the window. "Street's clear." He put his hand at Dani's back.

"Cutter... key's." Matthew hurled another set at Cal. "Take the Jeep. No devices on it."

Jay hadn't expected Dani's agent to be quite this welcoming.

"Here." Matthew peered out the side door, then reached back to hand Dani the keys to his car. "You'll need to drive."

"Me?"

Jay gave Matthew a closer look. His eyes were half-lidded and he leaned heavily against the door frame. His face was as pale as his hair. "You need medical care, man."

"Soon." The word was a mere whisper. "Let's

go." He ran out and to the driver's side of the car. His gun in his hand, he stood behind the door while Dani climbed in.

Jay let Cal lead him to the black Jeep Renegade next to Cal's sedan. He climbed aboard and strapped himself in. "You sure you want to do this?" His partner hadn't been a fan of Dani's. Not since he learned that she was keeping secrets. Even before he knew what the secrets were, as far as Jay could tell. "I know you want me away from Dani."

"I don't want you away from Dani." He backed out of the drive, in pursuit of the silver car. "I just don't want to see you hurting again."

Shifting gears, he sped down the quiet road. "Besides, this isn't about Dani. This is about capturing a man who violates children and enslaves women. This is about stopping a monster. And I'm all over that."

"All right, then." Jay put his eyes on the silver car in front of them, but a troublesome detail knotted itself into the edges of his brain. "There's something strange about that call you got."

"The one to our tail?"

"A nagging thing."

"Like an inconsistency?" Cal sped through a yellow light and drew closer to Dani.

"More of a bothersome coincidence. I don't like coincidences." At all. Ever. "I don't even believe there are such things."

"Are we talking spiritually or physically?"

"Both." Jay tugged his phone out of his pocket. "Why did you get that call then? Right after you took the call to me from Sam Bell?"

"How could they be monitoring your calls?"

"Nothing that's happened has been spur of the moment. Think of the Dallas shooting. That was planned moment by moment. The shooter knew how long it would take to get all the off-duty police on site. He knew to be at the perimeter near the downtown station, the obvious spot for the control center. He knew me." Jay shook his head. "It took weeks of planning."

"Your point?"

"My phone." He slipped off the back panel and pulled out the battery. If there was something there that wasn't supposed to be, he'd never know. Computers and software, he could manipulate, but not phones. "I lost it for several hours last week."

"You think it was snatched?"

"Yeah. I didn't think about it at the time. I'd met Ty for breakfast at the Dalrock Diner and realized I'd left it at home."

"So? That's not the first time you've done that, Jay." Cal sped through a yellow light and caught up with Dani.

"Yeah, but I'd plugged it in the night before and slipped it into my backpack." The memory came back a building block at a time. "And yet, I found it beside my bed."

"Simple. You set it as your alarm and forgot."

"I'm probably one of the few people who still use an actual alarm clock." Jay shook his head. "I couldn't help but wonder, with all the stuff in Tasha's email, why one innocuous note got tagged."

"I thought your security program tagged it." Cal turned in behind Dani onto a two-lane highway running southeast.

"No, the program missed it entirely. If Tasha hadn't called, I'd have never known that Dani contacted her."

"So, you think someone was monitoring the

calls?"

"Monitoring the phone. Tasha called me, but I put in the coordinates to the library and used the GPS."

"Has to be a really good hacker to have dug that out. Okay, we need to assume your phone is compromised. What are we going to do about it?" Cal pulled closer and flashed his lights at the silver sedan. Dani pulled to the shoulder and Cal pulled in behind him.

Jay rolled down his window. "We need to make sure we're not being tracked. Can you give me the address?"

Matthew leaned over with some effort. "I'll text it to you."

"No." Jay and Cal spoke at the same time.

"Dani, let me have your phone." Jay put his arm out the window.

Dani glanced at Matthew, then clicked through some keys and put the phone in Jay's hand. "I turned the lock off."

"Thanks. Matthew, text Dani the address. We're dumping our phones. Just in case."

"Phones? Plural?"

Jay ignored his partner's comment.

"Good thinking." Matthew straightened, and Dani pulled back onto the road.

Cal gave her room, then did a U-turn on the road.

Jay opened the settings on his phone and deleted his calls and texts. "I saw a truck stop a couple of miles back."

"You got a plan?"

"Yeah, but I'm thinking we're getting short on time about now." Jay cleared the cache from his map app, along with several others, and uninstalled them. Then he took Cal's phone and did the same with it.

After several miles, Cal pulled into the large parking lot. "What can I do?"

"Go get some duct tape. I'll meet you at the front door."

While Cal hoofed it into the store, Jay eyed the trucks in the lot. This late, most the trucks were staying for the night, but a couple of drivers milled about. One came out of the store right behind Cal and headed for a red cab with a grocery store logo emblazoned across the side of the truck and trailer.

Jay took the tape from Cal and strapped the two phones together. Then he tore off another long piece and sidled up to the red truck. The engine had already been idling, and roared as the driver shifted into gear.

Jay backed off a few steps in case the driver felt the need to back up, but the truck had a clear path to the exit.

The hauler roared again and crept forward a few feet. Jay dashed for the bumper and tucked the phones on the narrow step, wrapping the tape twice around the bumper as the truck accelerated. By the time he'd finished securing the bundle to the bumper, he was sprinting, but he shoved the end down firmly on the top of the phones. He ducked into the brush at the side of the lot as the truck pulled onto the road and leaned over his knees trying to slow his heartrate. This would work. It had to.

"I'm impressed." Cal stood leaning against the Jeep's hood. "I haven't seen you run like that since that chase after the kid who tried to steal your computer."

Jay huffed, unable to reply. He put his hands

on his head and tried to breath.

"We better get out of here in case our friendly tail is closer than we think." Cal climbed into the Jeep.

Jay stumbled around the vehicle and crawled into his seat. "I've got to start a better workout regime."

Cal let out a bellowing laugh. "I'd rather have a donut."

Marji Laine

Chapter Twelve

"How's your head?" Dani kept her eyes on the pavement in front of her.

"Sore." He twisted in his seat and glanced out the back window. "Ow. Not as bad as my butt. Forgot about the glass all over this seat."

"Oh, no. Are you hurt?"

He turned much slower, much more gently, to face the front glass. "Probably, but you're not going to help me, thanks." He pulled his briefcase out and opened it. "Patrick will be bringing two other agents with him." He took a deep breath and let it out.

"Are you going to be okay?" Something about

the shooting that afternoon nagged at her.

"Yeah. They should be there before us." He wiped his hand over his forehead and foraged through the case. "At least that's the plan if Patrick made good time collecting the key."

At least the man wasn't driving her Jeep anymore. Dani shuddered at the thought. And he'd had it for so long, too. Where in the world had he gone? He should have been at the house about the same time as she and Matt, even with Matt's insane speeding after they'd been shot at.

"And you need this." He pulled out a smaller case.

"What is this?" Not likely that she could get a good look at it, driving and all.

Some latches clicked and he lifted the lid. "The gun I got you when we came here."

Ice laced up her spine. "I don't do guns." Even though she'd learned how to shoot in high school, after her experience she hated the sight of them. "I told you that when you first brought it to the house."

"Look, I understand. Considering what happened to your dad, I don't blame you." He started fiddling with the gun. "But you will carry this one from here on in."

She clenched her jaw and fought her natural tendency. Her father and Robert both had a habit of ordering her around. "Matt, you can't force me to carry that gun."

"You're right, I can't." He leaned back in his seat. "I can't *make* you do anything. But I *can* tell you that Robert and his men are likely already in town."

"You really think so?" The ice spread across her shoulders. Was this it? Would she be face to face with Robert again?

"I do. And as good as I am, there are no guarantees." He withdrew the gun and shut the case. "And if your former fiancé gets through me somehow, this gun may be your only means of survival."

Her stomach knotted, but she remained silent.

"I know you've had training."

Of course, she'd had training. From early on. "My dad used to take me to the gun range every Thursday morning before school. I learned to dress an AK47 when I was a freshman in high school, and I even won a target-shooting award the next summer."

"So, you know how to shoot. There's no reason--"

"But I won't shoot. Not at a person. Not ever. I don't even like looking at guns anymore." The image of her father on the ground in a pool of his own blood flashed before her eyes. How could Matt even suggest that she carry such a weapon?

"Sammi, have you ever thought about what might have happened if you did carry a weapon? If you'd had a gun in your purse when you heard your dad and Robert fighting?"

She drew in a ragged breath. "That's not fair."

"There is no fair." Matt's volume rose and he straightened. "There's a man out there trying to end you like he ended your dad. He was only using you, tooling you to get to the detective who had started breathing down his neck." His determined declaration seemed to take most of his energy, and he sagged back against the seat.

He was right, though. Robert said he loved her, even asked her to marry him, but all he wanted was to get close to her dad. They'd had numerous conversations about her father. What he did and when. Where he met with friends. And how Robert could get into his good graces, a difficult feat even before she'd moved in with the man, but next to impossible after that.

Dad hated him. At least, that's what she'd believed. It was probably well-placed mistrust. Robert simply wanted something to hold over Dad's head to keep him from discovering the depth of Robert's enterprises.

But that day. That horrible...

"If you'd had a gun, your dad—"

"Don't say it." She hadn't meant to shout. But for him to even think that... to imply.... The road in front of her wavered and blurred. Her dad hadn't wanted her to have anything to do with Robert. Threw a fit when he learned she was seeing him. If she'd had her gun... *Oh, God, it was my fault. On so many levels. Why did I walk away from him and from You?*

"Regardless of the past, you have to carry this now. It could mean the difference between life and death." He laid his hand on the closed case. "Not only yours."

If something happened to Jay from all this

mess, she'd never be able to forgive herself. Though she was already in that spot with guilt over her dad. She clinched her hands around the steering wheel. "This is all my fault. First my dad, and now you and Jay. I'm the one who brought them here with my stupid email."

"I wish you had told me about that." He sounded half-asleep.

"Since Jay and I started seeing each other, you griped about our doomed relationship. I didn't want to hear that I would never see him again and would be better off to get over it. There's no getting over the hole in my heart that formed the moment we drove away and has been aching every moment since then." She had no business fussing at him in his state, but the words poured out. "You could never understand."

"I understand more than you think." Matt's soft reply startled her. "My wife's name was Constance."

Wife? He'd been married? "I didn't know." Didn't ask or bother to dig out of her own interests and problems. So much for being a different person than the Sammi Fellows who only thought about herself. Wait, *was*? "What happened to her?"

He was quiet for several minutes. Had he fallen asleep?

Suddenly he cleared his throat. "One of our cases was particularly messy. The client was forever taking advantage of his protection, making connections with shady individuals who had no compunction over sharing all they knew about him, for a price. The guy made a bundle with one con after another. I was brought in to strike fear into him. By then, he'd not only come to the notice of the syndicate he was trying to avoid, but he'd also conned the wrong people once too often. Still, he neglected to contact me until his life had been threatened. I guess he thought things would blow over, but it was only a matter of time before either his marks or his old syndicate buddies got to him. Unfortunately, that time came right after he called me, running for his life. I wasn't far from him, but Constance was with me and had to come along."

"Oh, no." Dani tried to concentrate on the highway.

"The guy ended up dead. The syndicate boys got off, and some sucker who lost his life savings went to jail for murder. I didn't realize that an errant bullet had hit Constance until after the police had arrived to take over the scene. By then, she was gone."

"I'm so sorry." Her voice broke into a whisper.

"It's been a while. I'm all right." He breathed in deeply. "And I know how much you care about Jay."

"I know. Impossible relationship."

"That's not what I was going to say. Obviously, he cares about you. He came all this way."

He'd shown her his love in so many ways, but this was probably the first time Matt had seen it.

"I preach the need for secrecy, Sammi, but the guy already knows everything that can put you in danger."

"What are you saying?"

"You need to be honest with him. Fully honest."

"I can't tell him about Daddy." Or about Robert either, though she suspected he already knew about that part of her fallen life.

"It's going to keep eating at you if you don't."

Being without him for almost three months had already torn her up. But this wasn't only about her.

Maybe if Jay knew the truth, the whole truth, it would be easier for him to turn his back and walk away. And walking away from her would be the safest thing he could do.

Marji Laine

Chapter Thirteen

"You sure this is the way?"

Jay looked at the GPS overview once more as his partner guided the car up the narrow grade. "This thing has us going to the other side of the butte."

Even with Cal's brights clicked on, it was hard to see the one lane track. Thankfully, the shoulder was wide, even if it was covered with scrub brush and mesquite trees making strange shadows. The moonless night didn't help, but the stars were gorgeous so far away from the lights of Abilene.

He glanced at the stoic face of his partner. Not even a toothpick broke the serious set to his jaw. He could almost hear his partner's thoughts. "You don't like this."

Cal hummed something tuneless, like he answered the question without opening his mouth. Then he wiped his hand across his nose and sniffed. "No. I mean we did what we came to do. We should be going back home."

"You wanted to stay back at the store. What changed?"

"I got all caught up in the game." Cal snorted. "But this isn't a game, Jay. The men in this aren't playing. They're fighting for their lives, as wicked and cruel as they may be."

"I know. And I know I've put you in danger. That wasn't my intention."

Cal shook his head. "Shoot, son, it's not like we haven't been through this type of thing before."

"Yeah, but I don't want you to risk your life for someone you don't even like that much.

Cal glanced at him. "That's the point. This isn't about the girl. When I think of the young people this monster has been victimizing..." He put his eyes back on the road. "But I'm not sure we can win this fight."

"Then go home. Just drop me off at the house and go. I can take a flight or rent a car when this is all over."

"You think you'll be getting to the 'all over' point of this? I mean, do you think there's really a chance that Dani will be given an 'all clear'?"

"I hope so." Though Cal was right about the chances even if they were able to control the initial meeting.

The road took a jig, then passed through an open gate. Cal directed the car over guardrails and a formidable gate closed behind them. "I don't dislike Dani. But she's done nothing except lie to you since you met her. She's kept her secrets and put others in danger because of them."

Jay clenched his teeth against the tirade he wanted to unleash on his partner.

"I like her. I do. But you can't let yourself go blindly after her without admitting her flaws. Denying them doesn't help you and won't give you a lasting relationship. Believe you-me, I've got the scars to back up what I say."

"Dani's not like your ex-wife, Cal." Hopping from one affair to another, Cal's ex had told so many lies, she simply couldn't keep them all straight.

"No, but she's not the perfect woman you have sitting up on that pedestal. That's a treacherous place for her to be and an accident waiting to happen for you, too."

Jay stared at the grove of trees through which they drove. Lights on various trees gave a well-lit feel to the area, but they didn't dispel his own frustration. He'd excused and justified everything Dani had said or done. He didn't think she was perfect, not really, but maybe he needed to be a little more honest with himself. "I doubt I'll have anything to do with her after this." She would probably go back to Sacramento anyway.

"That's not the answer either." Cal huffed. "All I'm saying is you should pray before you talk to Dani about returning to Dallas."

"I'm not asking her to come back."

"And you've prayed about that?" Cal wasn't letting the point go.

Jay settled a little lower in his seat. He hadn't. He'd been disgusted with what he'd learned about her past. Seemed the woman he'd loved wasn't at all what he believed. "I can't imagine the Lord would want me to condone her behavior."

"And I can't believe you can be so two-faced."

"Two-faced?" The word came out as an explosion. What in the world was Cal talking about?

"Yes. With one you tell the girl you love her, try to propose and everything. But the minute you learn something about her that is ugly, you're ready to walk away."

"This isn't a little issue."

Cal didn't back down. "No. It's more like the woman caught in adultery and flung down at Jesus feet. He didn't condemn her, but you feel you should?"

"You don't understand."

"*I* don't understand?" Cal snorted. "I know what it's like to be lied to, Jay. The hurt you're feeling, betrayal. Especially because of the type of lies she told you. The omissions. Letting you believe that she was something that she wasn't."

Jay let his chin drop. Cal did know the ache. But even in his disgust over the matter, the person he wanted to talk to most was Dani. "I feel like I've lost a piece of me."

"I get it. I still feel that pain sometimes. But I've seen the way she looks at you, Jay. This has been tearing her up, too."

Had it? "She could have told me."

"And put you in the same danger she was in. The same danger you're in right now. Huh-uh. No way a woman truly in love would have done that." He turned in Jay's direction. "And she didn't."

Jay didn't answer. Scenes of their times together threaded through his mind.

"You're all over the place right now, spurred on by emotions. Love, anger, disgust, hurt. Your head can't give you the right answer. You need to pray about your next step before you take it. Dani going back to Dallas might not be the best thing, for either of you."

Cal surely hadn't intended to imply that Jay shouldn't go back to Dallas, but his words twisted around a seed that had been planted when he'd gone home to introduce Dani to his parents. "I've been thinking about that a lot."

"Taking Dani back with you? I know you're serious about the girl, Jay. You don't have to tell me that."

"No. I still don't know about that. I'll take your advice, though, and pray about it. Assuming we get out of here. But I've been thinking over the last couple of months, maybe I should go back home. Back to Marseilles."

Cal stayed silent for a few minutes. Jay could barely see his profile in the dark car, but his jaw looked set.

"You're a cop, Jay. And you're good at it. This girl has you rethinking the calling the Lord placed on your heart?"

Still felt strange hearing Cal talk like that. Strange but wonderful. "This doesn't have anything to do with Dani. And I want to stay in law enforcement, but my folks are getting older, you know."

"That trip you took home."

"Yeah." The Fourth of July celebration at his folks' place would never be quite the same after all that he learned a few months before. "My brother helps, but he's got a lot of... well, baggage. And my sister with her new baby, she and her husband aren't in a position to help Mom and Dad."

"Well, son." Cal's voice sounded considerably lower. "Things wouldn't be the same without you." He took a deep breath and let the exhale expand his cheeks before releasing it. "I've actually been thinking about taking early retirement. Or maybe transferring east, out near my brother's place. Quiet. Fishing. And the chance to spend some quality time with him while we can still abide one another.

Jay applied a tight-lipped smile, the best he could muster. "Sounds nice. Peaceful.

"Yeah, I can sure see why you'd want to go home to be near your family."

And be away from Dallas, especially a Dallas without Dani. Regardless of the ache in his heart, he couldn't deny he still loved her.

Cal pulled around a bush-lined curve and stopped in front of a multi-story, limestone mansion. "Of course, that assumes this isn't our own personal Alamo."

Jay took in the windowless building. A stone walkway connected various balconies, all with solid-looking wooden doors. The man had a point.

Chapter Fourteen

Jay sucked in a gasp as he entered the fortress. The lights of Abilene spread out across the open wall opposite the entrance. The formidable front of the mansion was like a squirrel tail on a chicken. The inside was nothing like the stoic facade. Where the front approach had only shutters, heavy wooden doors, and balconies, the back was almost solid glass with a wide porch dangling off the acute descent of the butte.

"Nice, huh." Matthew came in from what seemed to be a kitchen area with a water bottle in his hand. Dani was nowhere to be seen. "We use this safe house for some of our most difficult cases.

A virtual castle in the front, but the clients don't have to feel completely closed in. Would have brought Dani here earlier, but the place was being used until last week."

Jay thought back to several high-profile court cases. Which one of the witnesses had needed protection? "The Comstock case?"

Matthew arranged a pillow on the sofa, but glanced up at him in silence.

"I guess you can't tell me either way."

The man gave a flat smile, abandoned the sofa, and moved to an overlong dining table set to look out through the glass.

"Some view you got here." Cal had his back to both of them, staring out toward the deck. "Too bad you don't have the perspective to watch anyone approaching the house."

"Oh, you mean like this?" Matthew sat at the head of the table and flipped open a small panel. The wall next to the kitchen entrance jumped to life with at least two dozen monitors, all showing various locations inside the house, the grounds, and even on the road that approached the grounds. "This place has all kinds of sweet tech."

Jay spotted Dani on one of the monitors. She knelt in front of a chair, her shoulders shaking with sobs. He pointed to the screen. "Where is she?"

"Give her a moment." Matthew touched something and the screen again took on the appearance of a normal wall. "She'll be down when she's ready."

Taking a deep breath, Jay paced the length of the great room.

"Speaking of tech…" Cal took a drink from his water bottle. "…I have an idea."

The front door burst open. Jay jumped and reached for his gun. He noticed Matthew already had his out and aimed. Cal had hit the floor, but bobbed up in a second behind the couch with his weapon at the ready.

The same blond guy who had visited the house in town froze mid-stride, halfway through the entrance. "You wanna take it easy?"

"That's what the intercom is for." Matthew tucked his gun away in a front holster.

"Why should I have to announce myself? I'm the one who opened the place up for you." The man snorted. "I was only going to report that the perimeter is secure. I left Pack and Harrison at the gate.

Matthew glared at him for a second, then turned toward Jay. "I know you've already sort of met, but let me formally introduce you to Patrick Staller. He's been my look-alike for that past couple of months. Patrick attended classes with Dani while I worked with the department on her case and possible options."

Jay nodded to the guy, probably five years his younger and lucky that he would see another birthday.

"I was sort of Candy's second husband." He sneered. "Though I'd rather have been bedding a rattler."

Again, he was lucky to see another birthday after that crack.

"That's enough." Matthew gave the man a different look, a strange look. Almost full of suspicion. "Sit down, Patrick." Matthew motioned him into a seat with his back to the glass. He nodded for Jay to take the seat next to him. "With the resources we have here, we could take down a small army, but we have to have a plan in effect or we have no chance." His eyes drifted to Jay for a moment before settling back on his junior agent.

"Agreed." Cal sank into the chair next to Jay. "That's why I have a little present for you." He pushed the cell phone toward Matthew.

"Well, that was stupid." Patrick practically spat the word and stood up. "You already know someone's been tracking you, and you bring that thing here?"

Silence filled the room. The kid hadn't been in on any of their conversations about tracking.

"Patrick, sit." Matthew didn't even look at him but kept his eyes on the phone and addressed Cal.

The younger man sat back down.

"You disposed of your phones?" He glanced at both of them.

Jay nodded. "This one belonged to our friendly tracker."

"You're crazy to bring it here." Patrick stayed in his chair, but his face reddened.

Matthew ignored him and picked up the phone. "And properly turned off, I see."

"Wouldn't want them to find us before we were ready." Cal sat back in his chair and put his hands behind his head.

Matthew smiled, a little broader than before. "Indeed." He snapped off the back of the device and pulled the battery. "Looks clean." He slipped out the card and inserted it into a dedicated reader. "This should tell us quite a lot."

The monitor which had been focused on Dani now bounced up with a scroll of data: numbers, coordinates, email addresses, and passwords. Could it really be this easy?

Dani joined them at that moment. Her cheeks showing a slight blush from her emotion, but otherwise as beautiful as ever. Even with her purple-tipped hair. Jay stood, but she avoided his eyes and turned to the wall where the data continued to scroll. "Hey, wait, stop. Something there looked familiar."

"You're not an agent, so you don't give orders, Candy." Patrick leaned back in his chair as though he wanted to put his feet on the table.

Jay was tempted to knock him over. He forced himself away from the table, still gazing at the wall of monitors. The distance between him and the pseudo surfer-dude-agent might just save the guy's nose. Especially if he kept leaving it over his opening mouth.

"I hate that name. Call me Dani. At least I'm used to that one."

Matthew had stiffened about the time Dani called out and hadn't turned away from the scroll on the wall. "I can't stop the data. It's downloading it from this phone. What did you see?"

"It was a number, but I'm not even sure I saw it right." She sat in the corner of the couch and cast a glance toward the table. "Probably didn't."

The stream stopped abruptly. "There." Matthew pointed at the screen. "That's the origin of the last call."

"How did you get that? It was a private number." Cal moved to the chair next to Matthew, looking over the console.

"I couldn't explain the tech even if it was allowed." Matthew almost cracked a smile. "But I sure like using it." He clicked on the number and a menu opened. "If your caller has his phone turned on." He clicked the link and a map flashed onto the screen. "And he does." Matthew joined Jay at the wall. "Right here."

Cal followed him. "Looks like our little trick worked, Hunter."

Sure enough, the blip on the screen seemed to be slowly creeping south on State Highway 283.

Matthew went to a desk against the corner and picked up a file. "When the time comes, we'll be able to watch them all the way in."

"When's that time you're talking about?" Jay glanced at Dani, still in the corner of the couch. The sooner they could get her out of here, regardless of where she decided to go at that point, the better her chances of returning to some semblance of normalcy.

"I think a few hours and we'll be ready. Would like to have the thugs cuffed and dropped in the local jail before dawn." He went back to the table and motioned to Cal. Cal sat back down.

"Dawn?" Patrick jumped to his feet again, this time knocking his chair backwards. "You need to delay until at least daylight."

Matthew punched in something on his phone. "My task force, Patrick. My plan."

Was the man texting? Who and why now?

"Have you gotten clearance for this?" Patrick

paced to the wall and stared at the map for a moment.

If he kept it up, Jay wouldn't be the only one who wanted to knock him down. Matthew ignored him and collected a file from a desk in the corner. "Here is a schematic of the property."

"I'm telling you, this is wrong." Patrick paced once again before a man's voice came over the intercom.

"McKray here."

"Come." Matthew stood as a man in covert-ops dress entered through the front. "I think you're right, Patrick." The man turned to face his junior agent. "I do need to make an adjustment to my plan. McKray and you will cover the gate. Dawson will move up to the house."

Patrick eyed the one called McKray. Bigger and taller than Matthew, he could twist Patrick, who was closer to Jay's size, into a pretzel.

"Fine." With the one word, he left the house in the company of the black-clad agent.

"Matt, about that—"

"We need to move on." Matthew's gaze flicked toward Dani as he reseated himself.

Jay's internal alarms had already reacted to the younger agent. Now, he got the distinct feeling that Matthew didn't trust him as far as Dani could throw him. Probably, letting on would be dangerous at this point. What were the options? "Are you sure? Maybe it would be a better idea to leave… certain people behind and move Dani."

Cal caught Jay's glance. "We could always subdue… someone… and tie them up so they couldn't… can't complicate matters."

Matthew had glanced at both men, then looked at Dani once more. "I noticed Patrick's phone number in the data scroll, too."

"It was so fast. I wasn't sure I'd seen it." Dani lowered her gaze to the floor in front of her.

"I think he was the one who shot at me this afternoon." Matthew suddenly looked about ten years older.

Dani jerked her head up. "That's why he took so long to get to the house."

"And why he knew something about the tracking devices. He'd not been in on any of those discussions."

"Do we leave then? Now?" Jay wished he'd

have flattened the guy when he had the chance.

"This place is meant as a fortress, hard to access and easy to defend." He wiped his hands down his dark pants. "We were planning to make a stand here anyway, but instead of just before dawn, it will likely be only a couple of hours." He pointed to the blinking light on the map, still moving slowly.

Wouldn't those tracking it realize by now that they were following the truck?

Matthew's phone buzzed and he walked into the kitchen.

"This really is our Alamo." Cal went back to the glass overlooking the lights of Abilene. "Shouldn't stay, but can't leave."

"We've got a lot of tech toys they didn't have back then." Jay spread out the property map again. "Cameras and heat sensors in the trees."

Dani stood and wandered closer as Matt returned. "What are those?" She pointed to a trio of flat lines in front of the driveway gate.

"Lasers that will trip an alarm. The agents at the gate house will know that someone is coming three miles before they reach the gate." Matthew laid his phone down. "And we have some back up coming. It will take a while for them to get here, but several more agents should put this firmly to our advantage."

"What about Patrick?" Dani eyed the agent.

"McKray is wrapping him up right now. He won't be a problem."

Dani went back to the couch.

Jay sat next to his partner and scanned the pages that Matthew showed as he talked. He went through the steps and expectations. Jay's tension eased. This place was the even more formidable than the fortress originally looked. As long as Dani stayed in the safe room near the center of the house, she'd be in no danger. And the rest of them would be able to disarm and control every possible attack with the military-grade tools available to them. Reminded Jay of a new video game he'd seen advertised. This situation had higher stakes, but better odds.

Matthew stood and rolled up the maps and pages. "I'm going to go check the gate." He set the papers down at the corner desk and moved to the front door. "I'll be back in about fifteen minutes."

He pointed toward the wall where one of the agents paced in front of the closed ornate metal. Then he left.

"Guess this conference is over, huh?" Cal stood and walked toward the kitchen. "If we've only got an hour or two, I'm gonna do a little fridge raid. Wanna join me?"

Jay held up his hand. "Gonna pass on that." He glanced at Dani again. Poor thing looked exhausted. "Hey." He got up and moved in her direction. "How about some air?"

Her eyes met his, but she seemed frozen for a moment. Then she got to her feet and preceded him through the sliding door to the porch.

His mind screamed at him, but his heart hoped this would give them a chance to reconnect.

Marji Laine

Chapter Fifteen

Dani stiffened when Jay's hand touched her back at the glass door. How often had she longed for his touch, to see him again, but not now. Not like this. Not when she had so much to tell him. Things he was going to hate. Hate her for the things she'd done. The things she'd been.

He pushed the door wide with his other hand and guided her onto the wide wooden porch. Her tennis shoes made muffled tapping noises on the surface followed by the louder thunk of Jay's hiking boots. The smell of dust mingled with pine. Must've been the material for the porch, because the only trees for miles were thick masses of mesquite. Not so much above them toward the summit of this tabletop, but knots of the trees blocked out everything below them all the way to the highway.

Funny, she hadn't noticed the house from the highway, but then there were probably two or three miles between them. All she could see of the highway were headlights, and those only barely. From the cars perspective, the porch probably blocked the lighted windows, so there was little to be seen.

Jay leaned against the railing on her right. He stood in silence, not even touching her, for some time.

Oh, God, how am I going to tell him all of this? She gazed at the sheen of stars in the moonless sky and waited for the Lord to answer her. Surely, He would. Jay was His servant and devoted to Him. God couldn't want the man to be hurt any more than he already was. Would that he'd never laid eyes on Dani. She was trouble for him from almost their first meeting. She'd gotten him hurt, shot, almost killed more than once. And for what. She had nothing to give him. Not even hope. Only the assurance of his impending broken heart.

What a piece selfishness I am.

Shutting her eyes, she asked for forgiveness again, not only for hurting Jay, but for all of her decisions, those done in ignorance as well as the ones she did with full knowledge of her actions. How long could she stand here under the weight of her guilt? But was unloading on Jay, telling him everything to simply ease her own burden fair? Maybe she shouldn't tell him anything after all.

"I know about Robert, Dani." He barely moved a muscle, but he might as well have set off a bomb.

She looked out over the dark landscape. She'd lived in that darkness, deep in her soul, for far too long. And her silence threatened to pull her right back in. Seemed God had given His answer. "I'm not proud of what I've done. And I have no excuses. I dated Robert against my father's wishes, and when Dad tried to expound on the crimes he claimed against Robert, I left home completely." She was no prude, but explaining this to the man she loved broke her. Her volume lowered to almost a whisper. "I moved in with Robert. Lived with him almost a year."

The light from the windows revealed a twitch in the muscle on Jay's jaw. "Yeah. Cal told me you were engaged."

She had no animosity toward Cal. The man had been a good friend, even better to try to protect Jay from the likes of her. "Yes. And I knew the police were always trying to pin things on Robert. He was an importer and had a huge warehouse and several stores. They were always accusing him of smuggling drugs or stolen material. Once there was a question of gambling and running some high-dollar operation. Like something out of the old mafia stories. Robert wasn't mafia. But he was a very wealthy businessman, even if he didn't have a stellar reputation. When we went out, the people at the clubs and restaurants always bent over backwards for him. At least that's what I told myself."

"You loved him?"

The words sank in. No, she hadn't loved Robert. She'd loved the things he bought her and the way people catered to her when he was around. She'd loved the big estate and the travel and luxuries she'd never even imagined.

"I was fully of the world. Enjoying all the luxury and respect that Robert's ample bank account could fund." She took a breath and looked his direction. "But no, I was using him as much as he was using me. And he was using me. As long as I was in his control, my father insisted on irrefutable proof of his involvement in something criminal before he would act upon it. His team came close, but were never able to pin anything on Robert."

Jay turned to look at her then. Pain etched his face. "You sound proud of him."

Turning away, she blew out a deep exhale. That couldn't be further from the truth. "I was blind. I believed that the police were completely confused. Robert had enemies in state offices that were twisting the truth and putting him under suspicion. And everyone around me confirmed my belief. Even the pastor at my church encouraged me to stand by Robert. That the truth would come out and exonerate him." Poor man. He'd been completely deceived as well.

Jay studied the rail in front of him. "So, what happened? How did you figure out he was the crook your dad had always claimed?"

She swallowed hard. "Dad got the proof he needed. But he wanted to protect me and asked to talk to me. I agreed, but I was weary of him trying to convince me of Robert's guilt. I refused to come home. Instead, I agreed to meet him on a point above our house. Robert's estate. It was a pretty quiet place back behind the old barn where there used to be horses and tack." She stopped, reliving that day, those moments. What kind of person could...

"And? I guess you might as well tell me all of it, Dani." His voice had a coldness to it that she'd never heard. It sliced through her heart like a frozen dagger, but he was right. She needed to continue.

"I got there a little early, and I heard something in the stable. Sounded like crying. There were some broken slats near a trashed-out tractor, probably from some animal burrowing inside or escaping. I couldn't see very much because it was so dark, but there was a single bulb hanging. And around the room were women, girls really, chained against the wall by a wrist or an ankle. One was crying. Some were sleeping. Some stared into space."

The muscle in his jaw played again for a moment. "Trafficking."

"I don't know. I thought so. I was sick. I ran for the house to tell Robert what I'd seen, but he'd left." Her eyes clouded. "I thought he was mad because I'd agreed to meet with Dad."

"You told him about your meeting?"

Out of her periphery, Jay turned toward her with wide eyes. She dropped her chin as the darkness before her turned into an ominous kaleidoscope. "I truly believed Dad was wrong."

Dani struggled for a moment to regain some control. "At the most, Robert might have had some gambling going on somewhere. Possibly illegal trading, which would technically be smuggling. But I didn't even think he'd be so bad as to deal in drugs. This trafficking of human lives wasn't even on my radar. But I'd seen what I'd seen. Even then, I was sure that one of his men, maybe Tony Dimitriadis, was doing this behind Robert's back."

Not really. She'd had to talk herself into believing that. "I called the police, though, and reported what I'd seen and then headed back out there. After all, Dad was meeting me nearby. It galled me to tell him about the girls, but I was determined to do so, and he would need back-up."

"Is that how he died?" A gentler tone colored Jay's voice this time.

Dani steeled herself against it. He deserved so much more than her baggage. Besides, when she finished the story, he'd not have any semblance of kindness for her. "No. I never spoke to him. When I reached the place, I could hear Robert talking to him. Reasoning with him. I thought this might be the chance for Dad to set aside his anger and listen to the man."

She took a ragged breath. "And, God forgive me, I thought those women could wait a little longer. After all, my happiness was at stake." She choked on the words. All she'd cared about was her own comfort, even when it came to those poor women. She'd been more concerned about her conscience than the women themselves. "I was tired of Robert's pressure to get Dad off his back. Tired of Dad's insistence of Robert's guilt. If they talked it out, everything would be fine. Then they could find the women together and turn in Tony or whomever was responsible."

The view from her place on the porch disappeared. Instead, she was looking through the leaves of a thick bush, hugging the side of the rich forested area near Robert's property. A tear escaped and tracked down her cheek. "But Robert wasn't reasoning with Dad. He was giving him an ultimatum. And when Dad tried to talk through it, Robert raised a gun with a silencer and shot him." She gulped in air. "He shot my daddy as though doing a bit of target practice." Tears streamed now, and she didn't even bother to brush them away. "He wiped his hands on his jeans and headed back down the hill, whistling." Her voice broke. "Whistling!"

She'd been stunned, fallen back on her behind in the thick grasses. But she'd seen what she'd seen. With Robert out of sight, she'd rushed to her father's side. "Dad was dead. Robert was talking to someone, probably sending them to take care of... I ran. I made it to the house and grabbed my purse and keys and would've been gone if the police hadn't stopped me at the gate. They swarmed the place, but they arrested me and took me out fast. I could hear the gunfire as we drove away. I have no idea how many people were hurt or killed because

I refused to see the truth all around me."

Her tears had subsided, but a last one escaped and trickled down her cheek. "But I know of one who died. And it was my fault. As if I'd pulled the trigger myself."

There. Now Jay knew as well as she did that they could never have a future together. If only she'd been honest with him before. The man deserved so much better.

Chapter Sixteen

Jay gripped the rail in front of him so tightly, splinters cut into his palm. Dani's tears broke him. Her full story had Jay both horrified at her and hurting for her at the same time. "What happened to the women?"

"The detective in charge was my dad's former partner. He and Daddy had a falling out when I moved in with Robert. Naturally, he wouldn't tell me anything, but I did learn that they had all been smuggled north from Mexico. A psychologist that used to work with my dad told me they were being cared for."

At least there was something good out of all

the sorrow. A thought dawned on him, certainly from the Lord Himself. "You're a hero."

She gasped and faced him. "I killed my own father." She took a deep breath and looked at the railing again. "I am no hero."

"To those women you are."

"What about the others? The ones who'd been moved along the prostitution circuit while I was busy going to clubs and wine tastings and high-class parties and social events. What about the ones who are still tangled in that filth because I didn't want to look my gift horse in the mouth? I didn't want to spoil my fun by questioning the man who lavished me with expensive toys, baubles and exotic trips." She seemed to crumble as she spoke. "No. I'm not anyone's hero. I'm nothing but the spoiled brat who was finally caught, and was luckily not as technically guilty as others."

She turned her head toward him. "That's why Matt barely tolerates me. My only value is that I'll make a great tattletale. If they ever get Robert back in prison."

He had little response to that. She knew Matthew much better than he did, though he tried not to think of that. "Matthew wouldn't have gone to so much trouble to marry you if he didn't care a little." Probably more than a little.

Alarm filled her eyes. "There's nothing between us, Jay. It's not even a real marriage, only a document to hide me better."

He'd thought as much, but it was nice to hear. "I'm not judging you, Dani."

"You have every right to. I should never have gone out with you, Jay. I knew this would happen at some point. You don't deserve all this pain."

"And you do?" He let his finger trail down the sleeve of her sweater from her shoulder to her elbow. "Dani, we all make mistakes."

"Not like mine."

He tugged at her forearm when she would have turned away. "Just like yours. Selfishness, greed, laziness, ambition, there's nothing new under the sun." He caressed her arm with his thumb. "And you're as equally forgiven." He brushed a lock of black and purple hair from her face with his other hand. "Except by you. You have to forgive yourself."

She looked up at him then, her soft, chocolate

eyes brimming with hope. "But you don't forgive me... do you?"

Somewhere to the right of the porch, someone shoved their way through the overgrowth. "What did you do." Matthew's voice, charged with fury. Then the sound of someone landing a blow, fist against skin, probably a face.

Dani flinched.

"You should have listened." Another man. Was that the Patrick kid? How had he gotten away from McKray. "You couldn't be bothered. Always had to run things your own way. Well, I found someone who liked my ideas." The man practically hissed.

Dani's eyes widened and her mouth partly opened, she looked the picture of desperation. If Patrick had gotten loose, then Dani's fian... Robert might be here, she had to get to safety. The windows were still fully lighted downstairs and showed no signs of any security breach, but the screens lining the wall had disappeared. And where was Cal? Surely the man wasn't still in the kitchen after all this time.

Dani shivered next to him. Any moment

someone might come into the building and be able to see them. Not easily, but the lights from inside did reach the edge of the porch.

The edge... "Dani, over the side." His voice was barely a whisper and he pushed her toward the rail.

"What?" She held back, but her volume dropped to match his.

"You're a climber. Climb. Get to ground level and make your way to the highway. Go the most direct route, straight down the hill. I'll get to you when things are safe."

"Are you crazy?"

Again he pushed her. "Go, I'll hold onto you until you can map your strategy. But you need to get out of the light, now." He gave her another nudge.

She threw first one leg, then the other over the rail and paused for a moment with her weight on her arms. "Are you going to be all right?"

He stroked her cheek. "I'll come after you." Then, he grasped her wrists and leaned as far over the railing as he could, swinging her slightly toward the nearest stabilizer that reached to the web of pier and beams making the foundation for the porch and likely part of the house. She clasped onto the beam, making her climb look effortless. With her securely in her element, even in the dark, he straightened and pulled his gun from his waistband.

A shot rang out on the side of the house. *Lord don't let that have been Matthew.* He was the only one who really knew how to work the security gadgets. Especially with Patrick's betrayal. Resisting the urge to check on Dani, Jay took a step toward the darkest edge of the porch. Another shot rang out, burning through his shoulder.

The next thing he knew, he dangled over empty blackness, hanging from one of the slender boards that made up the railing.

"Jay." Thankfully, Dani had the presence of mind to keep her voice down.

"I'm all right." If he could make his other arm work. His grip loosened and his gun dropped, hitting the earth with a thump. Jay could make out the blur of a mesquite tree probably twenty feet below him, but what else might be there.

Footsteps on the porch above him. No place to hide. He could stay and get shot or drop and be left for dead. If the fall didn't actually kill him.

He glanced at Dani. She continued to climb downward without a hint of sound and barely any movement. She almost floated down the rafters. If only he could.

Lord, have mercy. He released his hold.

Dani bit her bottom lip, tasting blood, to keep from crying out as Jay fell. He was swallowed into the darkness, but as she descended, she could make out his blue shirt about twenty feet below the porch. No, it was a little more than that, but surely not so far that it could... She hurried down the rafters. He'd been right; this was an easy climb for her. Finally reaching the uneven ground beneath the house, she skirted a pile of rocks and a couple of boulders to get to Jay.

He'd been sort of cushioned by a mesquite tree. An even flatter than normal mesquite tree, now. She felt for his pulse and found it steady. And as she touched his neck, he groaned slightly. *Thank you, God!*

"He musta taken a nose dive. I seen him go over." A man's high-pitched voice that she didn't recognize. But if he hadn't been the one to shoot Jay, he was part of the group.

"Find heem and finish heem." That voice was unmistakable. Tony Dimitriadis had the deepest voice she knew. And a slight accent leftover from his early childhood in Greece.

Her shoulders gave an involuntary shake. Almost immediately, the bushes at the far right edge of the porch above her began to rattle. She couldn't stay there, but she couldn't leave Jay defenseless. She rolled Jay over, face-down onto the pile of rocks. He was out and made no sound. But what if he did come to?

She could *what-if* herself forever. Nothing would change what was going to happen. But she could do what she could. She slipped over the edge of the rock pile and dangled for a moment. This wasn't a simple rock pile. She was on the edge of a cliff. No mesquite trees with protruding roots to help her out here.

Wiggling to her right, she found a foothold and eased herself downward. Mentally, she stepped through Jay's instructions. Down the hill to the highway. She descended another two feet and turned to search for her next hold on a surprisingly sheer face.

But those instructions had been before Jay's fall. Before, she would have done anything he said. But now? He was still up there. Unconscious. Helpless.

What if Tony found him? He'd kill him without a second thought. Dani might have had doubts about the extent of Robert's evil, but never Tony's. The man was scary-tough. He bragged about hitting his "woman" and killing a troublesome friend of his. Jay's death wouldn't even rate a sneeze.

No. She'd stood by idly as her father died. She would never again simply let someone she cared for die. She would fight to ensure his survival, with everything she had.

Starting with her gun.

Rocks shuffled nearby, every sound piercing

through his head. Jay cracked open one eye. Where was he? His cheek rested on a hard, flat bolder. Oh, right. He'd dropped from the porch. But if he'd landed like this, he should be dead. Wiggling his fingers slightly, he ascertained that he wasn't dead.

He stifled a groan as a light played over the rocks nearby. A shadow with a flashlight moved closer, but he scanned the bushes and mesquite, ignoring the rocks at his feet. Apparently, Jay's shirt blended into the background well enough to camouflage him. As the shadow turned, a gun-looking profile came into view. Whoever it was, he meant business.

"Come on little girl." That voice. The high pitch of their tail from the afternoon.

The shadow examined a clump of bushes just above Jay's head and crept over the rocks until he stumbled over Jay's legs and caught himself against Jay's shoulder blade.

Searing pain lashed through Jay, but he bit the inside of his cheek and shut his eyes praying that the man would deem him already expired.

"Well." The light flashed across Jay's closed eyes. "Look at the tough guy." He leaned over Jay's face. "Not so tough now are you."

Jay squinted through the eye that was closer to ground level. The other man straightened and swung the flashlight backward like a tennis racket. *Now.* Jay tucked his leg and kicked out as the man moved toward him. He caught the guy square in the stomach, at the base of his ribs. The man let out a grunt and hurtled backward. His gun clattered onto the rocks near Jay while the guy thunked against one of the stabilizing piers. Another grunt and he crumpled.

Jay attempted to get to his feet, but his body didn't want to cooperate. His right arm sort of hung against his side, every movement slashing through him. The gun. If he couldn't fight, then he could hold his enemies off with the gun. He searched on the rocks nearby. It had to be close. He'd clearly heard it fall.

"You. You think you can do anything against a man like Torelli?" The tail was pushing to his feet, the flashlight still dangling from his hand.

Jay leaned forward and searched another area. His fingers touched cold metal, but the weapon evaded his grasp.

"You're nothing." The man moved toward him.

Something hard hit Jay in the head, and he reeled for a moment. The ground shifted and the rocks around him spun.

"And you're going to pay for leaving me in the desert."

The shadow of the tail loomed before him with a large stone in both hands.

Jay attempted to turn over to avoid the coming hit. He reached for the boulder next to him but touched nothing except air.

Chapter Seventeen

Dani could hear some man above her. Calling to her. She concentrated on shifting her hand-holds and placing her feet carefully. These sneakers weren't anything close to climbing shoes. For the third time, her foot slipped, leaving her dangling from the root system of a tiny clump of bushes she'd found.

Giving up on the soles of her shoes, she kicked one off and then the other, digging into the crevices with her sock-covered toes. She had to avoid a section made slick by the way her shoe had skidded on it, but a better foothold was on the other side of the knob in the cliff. If she could reach it.

Still clinging to the large roots with both hands, she reached for the foothold. She missed and swung out over the darkness beneath her. Her arms burned as she dragged herself back up to the root, a pseudo chin-up against both gravel and gravity partnering to shove her downward.

Again, with the toes of her left foot on a shaky hold, she swung her right leg out toward the little ledge. This time she touched it, but couldn't claim the spot. And again, she lurched into nothingness. The roots, her only tether, shifted slightly.

This wasn't working and failing again might just pull those roots completely out of the ground. There had to be another way to get back up the cliff. She lifted up on the roots and steadied her breathing, looking in all directions. No other option seemed the slightest bit feasible. But the foothold seemed too far away—even if only by a fraction of an inch. Still it was her only option.

The man above her started talking again. This time, he clearly spoke to Jay. Something about being a tough guy.

And Jay was helpless. What sort of self-serving creature would leave the man she loves like that to save her own skin? That was the old Sammi rearing her sun-like attitude. Well, she wasn't the center of the solar system, and Jay needed her.

Taking a deep breath, she swung her right leg back as she had before. She kicked it forward, this time pushing off with her left leg as well. The extra momentum carried her to the ledge. Still clinging to the roots, she paused, hanging over the crevice while her feet steadied. Bending at the waist, she glanced over her shoulder for another handhold and found one at the perfect height and only a couple of feet along the cliff side.

With her new handhold on a thick, rotting branch, she stepped up to the next level. A scuffle had erupted above her, urging her to hurry. But speed with climbing made for deadly errors. The other man began to talk to Jay again. Not a good sign. Finally, she was able to sink her hand into the thick mesquite tree at the edge of the cliff and pull herself up.

"This is for..." The strange man's voice had filled with rage.

Dani peered over the edge of the rocks and gasped. The man had a huge stone high above his head in both hands and stood poised to bash Jay's head in. With her right hand clinging to the tree, she struggled to pull her gun from her waistband with her left. Could she even take the safety off this way? She fumbled and almost dropped the weapon before finally gripping it firmly in her hand.

A shot rang out. Dani sucked in a desperate breath and tried to aim at the man. He wobbled forward, then teetered backward and crumpled into a heap. The boulder crashing down on him.

She had to get to Jay. Laying the gun on a rock, she hoisted herself over the edge of the cliff onto her knees. She picked the gun back up and ran to Jay, keeping an eye out for the shooter.

"I thought you'd be down here somewhere." A figure moved in the darkness to the left of the porch foundation.

Easing close to Jay, she huddled beside the pile of rocks. "Are you okay." Her voice barely carried past her own nose.

A slight groan was the only response.

"That better be you, Dani." The figure halted, his gun raising again.

"Cal." Jay's voice sounded as much a grunt as

his partner's name.

"I'm here, buddy." The figure moved forward.

Dani released the breath she'd been holding and slipped her weapon back into her waistband. She stood and leaned over Jay, checking his pulse. "Where are you hurt?"

"He hit me with something." Jay attempted to sit up and grunted again. His right arm hung in an awkward position.

"Lemme help you." Cal supported him on his left. "Was it your gun?" He picked up Jay's weapon from where it had landed a few feet away.

"No, smoother than that, but thank you for finding it." Jay attempted to reach for it, but only succeeded in moving his right hand an inch or so before grimacing in pain.

Dani took the opportunity to press herself against his arm, pinning it to his body. If only she had something to tie it in place. Blood drenched both the back and front of his shirt at the shoulder. She took a step and smashed her toe against something hard and distinctly metal. She reached for it. "A flashlight?"

"That was it." Jay leaned over. "Stunned me."

He listed heavily to his left. "I guess I still am a little. What's going on up top."

"Looks like three, maybe four men. I got out the kitchen window before they saw me and came down here." He glanced behind him. "Not sure what happened to Matthew or the others."

Dani stayed pressed to Jay's side and put her left arm around his waist. "How did anyone get through the security."

"A mole." Jay grunted as Dani and Cal lifted him to his feet. "From what I heard before I went over the rail, Patrick was indeed the turncoat we suspected. And apparently he was able to make contact after all."

"I knew I never liked him." Dani kept her voice low as she eased Jay a few steps up the side of the hill, the way Cal had climbed down. "But I know I heard Tony D. somewhere up there. There was a gun shot before Jay fell."

"Maybe one of the agents got him." Cal took a few short steps up the hill and pulled Jay upward.

Dani kept his arm as still as possible on his journey back up to the porch. "Doubtful." Not with only one shot anyway. "The man is a monster. A modern-day Goliath."

Cal paused under the think wooden beams that made up the porch surface. He leaned toward Dani and Jay. "Jay, you stay here." He pressed Jay's gun into his left hand. "Keep watch on the porch area. I'm going to create a diversion."

"What do I do?" Maybe she should keep the porch watch?

"My keys are in the kitchen. Climb through the window, grab 'em, and take my car back to town." Cal's gruff whisper dared her to argue.

"I can't leave." Was he ludicrous?

"Please, honey." Jay turned his dark eyes toward her. "Everything hinges on you staying safe. On you being able to testify about what you saw."

Leave? Run? How could she? *No, God. Please don't let this happen again.* "I can't. My dad and now you? Please don't ask it of me."

Jay blew out an exhale. "Dani--"

"No. This will work." Cal held up his hand. "Same plan, different goal. Dani, you get to the safe room."

"How is that diff--"

"From there, you can activate the security

options that Matthew discussed." Cal peeked over the edge of the porch. "It's clear. In through the kitchen." He pointed his finger at her.

She nodded. Cal peered over the edge once more. She looked into Jay's deep brown eyes. Would she ever see them again after this?

Cal climbed up the last few feet to the wood surface. Dani took the opportunity to press her lips against Jay's, then dashed up the slope to the side of the house. Gunfire broke out as she reached the open window, but she kept her calm. She took a quick glance into the room. Empty. After checking behind her, she hoisted herself onto the sill and in through the window.

Chapter Eighteen

Jay struggled to reach a position on the steep slope that allowed him to steady his left arm across the wood planks if he needed to take a shot. Of course, he'd likely only be able to hit ankles, but that could cause some damage if done well.

Shots rang out nearby, likely at the front of the house.

"Hey. Help. I need some help out here." Cal pounded on the glass door, then stumbled backward like he was drunk. "Hey, Patrick." He pounded again. If the guy was in there, that didn't bode well for Matthew.

The glass door swung wide, but no one came

out.

Cal stumbled away from Jay and leaned heavily onto the railing, reaching the shadows. "I've been shot."

The blond man poked his head out and looked in all directions as he took a tentative step outside. His gun at the ready, he eyed Cal.

"Help me… help me, Patrick." Cal went down on one knee.

"Not likely." The man took aim.

Jay fired with the best one-arm aim he could muster and caught the man in his shoulder. He twisted around, searching for the source of the shot. Jay fired again, unsure of where he aimed, but it must've connected. The man fell backward on the deck, his own gun flying from his grip. Cal was on him in a second. "You okay?" His whisper carried across the span of the porch.

Jay didn't answer. The shots would draw attention at any moment.

Cal checked the man's pulse, then he pulled something from the man's belt and scooted back to Jay at the side of the porch. "You nailed him in the kneecap with that second shot. Looks like he conked himself on the head when he hit the deck."

"And he's..." Jay had terminated a life before. He didn't relish doing that again. Even for the slime bucket who had been so insulting to Dani.

"Out." Cal stuck a thumb in the air, then touched a button on a handheld something. "Handy dandy little thing." A two-inch, square screen lit up. "But you can bet if one of them had it, the others do, too."

"What is that?" Several dots were lit and a couple of those were moving.

"Matthew told me about this. The trees are wired with heat sensing devices." He pointed to one moving blip. "That should be Dani in the house. These two are probably you and me."

Jay studied the screen. Several still dots were around the property. "And who are these?" He pointed at two other dots—one approaching the porch and another slowly creeping through the house.

"Trouble." Cal pocketed the piece. "You stay here. I'll try to find some cover."

The windows gave him none. "I've got your six." Jay scanned the area around him for any movement. The crickets had started chirping. That was a good sign. He ducked his head to look under the porch for a moment. He could see nothing directly under the beams, but the grassy area on the other side of the porch showed no signs of life either. Where were the other agents?

He looked back over the porch. Cal had made it across the lighted windows and put his back to the solid wall near the entrance to the porch from a garage perched beside the drive. His partner looked in his direction. Jay laid his gun down for a moment and waved the back of his fingers toward the house and back. No one had gotten past the porch on that side, so the blip they'd seen on the screen must've stopped along the side of the house.

A large bush stood hugging the side, just past the porch exit. Cal inched to look around the corner, his face camouflaged by the bush. His view likely blocked by it to, for the most part, but if he watched long enough, he'd know if someone was moving to his position.

Jay trained his eyes on the glass that ended at Cal's immediate right, well, his back now that he'd turned. A shadow flicked across the floor just inside the sliding door. Had Dani made it to the safe room?

His gut twisting, Jay struggled to gain a half-step higher on his incline. He could barely stand. Climbing to the side window that Dani used and hauling himself inside was out of the question. But he couldn't just stand there as a spectator.

In front of him, Cal put his back to the wall once again and fished the screen out of his back pocket. After giving it a look, he bent and shoved the box across the deck toward Jay. It hit him in the chest, and he didn't even have to catch it to get a clear view of a blip in line to intersect his own position along his side of the house. His cover from the undergrowth and the steep incline kept him safe for the moment, but the blip would run right over him within a few seconds.

Jay turned, easing his bracing arm off the porch. He slid a few inches down the incline before his footing caught again. With one arm, he aimed over the top of the tall weeds where a head had appeared.

Moving much slower at this point, the figure bent low and glanced around the corner for a second before readying his weapon. The guy never seemed to see Jay at all, though he was only inches away. Dropping to a knee, the man practically lay on the ground to bring his aim slowly into position. He probably thought he'd fade into the brush beside him, but Jay was part of that brush. Spinning his gun in his left hand, he brought the butt of it down on the man's left temple.

The man grunted and went slack, rolling onto his side. Jay tucked his own Sig Sauer into his waistband at his back, reached through the thick weeds and pulled the gun from the man's relaxed hand. He lifted it, waving slightly at Cal. His partner lifted his chin and pointed at the device still lying on the porch. Jay glanced at the blips. None of them really moving. Dani, or the blip that should be Dani, was pacing in what seemed to be the safe room. There was a blip inside the house, but Jay couldn't see any other shadows. Maybe the guy was in an upper floor? A couple of blips were ominously stationary near the entrance gate and another was on Cal's side of the house. Probably Matthew. A single blip was by the cliff below him, likely the guy Cal had shot. Jay's blip shown at the side of the porch, though he and the man so close to him had practically merged into one, especially with Jay so still. Except for the man in the upper region of the house, the other people on the property were either dead or otherwise incapacitated.

He straightened, stuffed the second gun in his waistband, picked up the device and pocketed it. Ignoring the pain in his shoulder, he forced his feet to propel him up to the wooden base of the porch. He took a breath and gave Cal a thumbs up. "Only the guy upstairs," he whispered and glanced again at the screen on the device.

As he watched, the still blip on Cal's side of the porch separated into two. The one remained stationary. The other... "Cal?" Jay caught a movement just beyond Cal's head before his partner stiffened.

"Lift your weapons," a low voice commanded. The face was hidden in the shadows, but the man's tone sounded desperate, almost reckless.

Cal lifted his thirty-eight. Jay slid the device into his front pocket and lifted his empty left hand.

"Throw it over the rail."

Cal did as he was told.

"You, too." Still in the shadows, and using Cal as a shield, the man lifted his gun to target Jay.

Jay held his right hand, palm forward, as far away from his body as he could get it. Only about two inches. With his left, he reached behind his back and slowly extracted one of the weapons he'd stored there.

"Toss it behind you."

He tossed it in the direction of the incline. "You're the only one left. You have nothing to gain."

The man snorted. "Where ees Sammi?"

"In the house." Cal pointed to the upper floors.

"I am not asking you. I am asking him." He nodded in Jay's direction. "Where ees the betrayer, cop?"

Betrayer? He peered into the darkness. The man stepped onto the porch.

This was Tony Dimitriadis. Jay recognized him from the pictures that he'd seen. Apparently, he was Robert's right hand. No wonder he thought of Dani as the betrayer.

Tony changed targets with his gun and pointed it squarely at Cal's forehead. Too close for him to miss, yet too far for Cal to hit the gun or tackle the man. "Where ees she?"

"Are you working on your own now, or is your boss still pulling the puppet strings?" He had to be out of his mind to kick an angry bull like that, but he couldn't send him after Dani. And he needed a few seconds to think of a plan.

"Where ees your little bed-warmer."

Jay flinched and resisted the fist that begged to be made.

"Tell me now, or your friend..." He cocked the weapon.

He wasn't playing. Jay could hear the gun going off in his imagination. Heartless. Cold. Without even looking, this man could end Cal's life and not have an eyelash flick of remorse.

"I gave her my keys. Sent her to my car." The fact that she'd refused to go was neither here nor there.

"No car drove out."

"That was the last that I saw of her." Jay kept his eyes steady on the man. All he needed was a second of hesitation, an instant of looking away so Jay could snag the other gun from his back.

His adrenaline pumped as he watched the man's eyes. "Ah, I see."

Jay didn't respond.

"And I believe you." Tony's eyes slid over to Cal.

Jay grabbed for his gun with his left hand while falling to his left knee.

The man turned and aimed at Jay.

"No." Cal leaped toward Dimitriadis, becoming an obstacle between him and Jay. A shot rang out. Cal continued his path but fell short of the hit man.

Jay caught Tony D. in his sight and pulled the trigger. The man fell backward, off the porch. Jay rushed toward him, determined to take the gun from his hand before he recovered from the shock, but his concern wasn't necessary. A red pool was forming in the center of the man's forehead, and his empty eyes stared into the sky.

Turning back to the porch, Jay knelt and tugged on Cal's shoulders. "Buddy." He turned him over and discovered a widening patch of red on the front of his shirt. "Hang on, Cal. I've got you."

"No, you don't." Cal's voice was a harsh

whisper. He gave a slight, skyward point of his finger. "He does."

"Always." Jay balled up the bottom edge of Cal's shirt and pressed it to the wound. "But I'm here to help."

"You gotta job to do, kid." He pointed again, this time toward the house.

A tear slipped down the end of Jay's nose. He kept the pressure on the wound with his one good arm. "Here, first." His voice broke.

"You ain't a doctor." He coughed and a trickle of blood escaped his lips. "Go be a cop."

"Cal."

The man patted Jay's hands. "You already gave me what I needed, son." He smiled. "I'm good." He took a slow breath and released it, his eyes closing. "I'm really good."

Jay squeezed his eyes shut. He didn't have words to say. Didn't even have words to pray. A groan rumbled low in his chest. Jay placed Cal's hands on the bundled shirt. "Press here."

"Go," came the whispered reply.

Jay once again moved off the porch to the grassy slope where Tony Dimitriadis had fallen.

Luckily, this incline was much smoother than the other side of the porch. Jay dug into the man's pockets for his phone and dialed 9-1-1. Giving the location and short explanation, he begged for ambulances and officers. Leaving the call live, he dropped the phone and picked up his gun. He hustled to the front of the house and pulled the device from his pocket. His was the only movement on the screen. Where was the other man?

Where was Dani?

As he watched the screen the blip that was him disappeared.

Chapter Nineteen

Dani paced for hours. Or it seemed like hours. For a while, she had a few monitors she could access. One at the front of the house gave her a view of the front porch and the gates. Two men lay near the drive, having taken stands against the ambush. She hadn't seen them fall, but they hadn't moved since she'd entered the safe room.

On the next monitor, she could see the main room of the house. She'd barely shut her metal door before Patrick had appeared on that screen. Thankfully, though he had to know about the safe room, he hadn't seemed to notice the wall behind him locking silently into place. Was Matthew the only other person who could reopen it? This whole defense might be a waste of time if Patrick noticed she was inside. She touched her gun tucked at her back.

A third screen showed Cal's antics on the porch, how he had lured the man toward him and how the man had been shot. That had been Jay's handiwork, of course. She prayed that Patrick didn't die from those wounds. Not only for his sake, but also for Jay's. He had such trouble living with guilt when he had to use his weapon.

The other three screens were dark for some unknown reason. Though she'd probably been the first person in the room for some time. According to Matt, the agents seldom used the place because of the risk of damage. Even when they did, like last week, it was more because of the elite status of the client rather than out of desperation. She paced and paused at the monitors again. Cal looked around the corner of the house, then that screen dimmed and went out.

What was going on? There had to be something wrong with the cameras. Maybe they hadn't kept them in good working order since they rarely used the building. It didn't matter, she knew nothing of electronics, so even if she had access to the devices, which she doubted, she'd have little chance to do anything like a repair.

She touched a button to give a scan of the heat signatures on the property. Matt had apprised her of that ability as they drove in. Cool tech. She identified Cal and Jay, then recognized the dot that must've been her. Another dot was in the room with her.

No, that couldn't be right. There was no one with her, but the image clearly showed a dot moving back and forth slightly. And standing right next to her.

The lights flickered.

Wait. Not next to her. Above her. In the electrical closet that opened to the attic.

Well, there was no way she was going to get stuck in this tomb with the lights going out.

She glanced at the monitor of the front room. That was clear. Completely. Easing the door open a bit, she inched out and returned to the kitchen. She vaulted herself onto the sink and dove out the window, rolling into a front handspring. Not something she would try from anything over waist-high, but it got her out of the lighted window and away from the easy view. Even with her gun, she wouldn't stay out here where who-knew-how-many of Robert's goons were looking for her.

A small tree grew too close to the stone building. Lots of handholds on the surface, though free-climbing at night wasn't her best thought. Still, the water meter clung to the side of the house. That would take her three-fourths of the way to a second-floor window sill. Had the building not been a veritable rock fortress, she wouldn't even try, but at least up there, she had a good chance to stay alive until other help arrived.

If it was coming. Which was a toss-up.

A shot rang out and she jumped. *God, please bless Jay.* She backed up several feet and took a running jump from the tree to the top of the post. She clung to the wall, looking like a stork with one foot on the round head of the meter. Her fingertips slid easily between the rough stone. This was the real thing, not some artistic facade. Thankfully she'd been able to tug off her sneakers earlier. The toes of her left foot found a sturdy pocket and she stepped up a good five inches. She searched for another handhold with her right and found one slightly right of dead center of the window above her. No matter.

Bracing herself, she let her right foot search and find a narrow edge. Too narrow. She glanced down and found the bump of an uncut stone sticking out several inches. It was smoother than the others, and a little higher than she liked to stretch, but doable. She found another handhold on her left and hoisted herself onto the rounded stone. She slipped for a moment and her heart thumped in her throat.

Don't look down. Even now, after so much climbing experience, she still had to remind herself. She gripped the wall till her fingers ached, probably impaling them on the sharp stones, but she was able to regain her stability. Reaching with her right hand, she clamped onto the window sill and pulled herself up. This one wasn't open like the kitchen window had been, but no matter. She didn't want to go back inside anyway.

She pulled her herself to her knees, and then stood, using the broad sill that stuck out. It was wide enough for a window box. Wonder if one had been there. The window was also edged with uncut rocks, some sticking away from the wall and others smooth against it. Had they built this place to be a free-climber's paradise? So many edges to choose from. Dani reached to the mild apex of the rooftop and inched her toes up the side of the wall until she could hoist herself over the edge.

Built like a castle in the front of the house, this roof only had the barest of grades. She pulled her gun from her waistband and skirted toward the front of the house where a large gable would give her some cover.

The lights inside the building went out as did the few that perched in some of the trees surrounding the driveway. *Thank you, Lord, that I wasn't in that tiny room when this happened.*

Something moved near one of the live oak trees that graced the front lawn. As she watched, a figure separated from the shadow of the oak and moved toward the front of the house. She was in full view of the person, if he chose to look. She gripped her gun, hating the feel of it, yet determined now to use it if she had to.

Footsteps thumped on the porch far beneath her. "Stop." Robert's voice spoke with deadly authority.

A spotlight of some sort pierced the figure who had been running. Jay. His right arm still bathed in blood. His gun in his left.

"You're the cop."

Jay squinted into the light. "I'm *a* cop." He said something else, but Dani stopped listening.

Robert would kill Jay. She couldn't live through that. Not again. Not after Daddy. Not another man she loved. No. With every individual thought, she inched further down the roof incline until her feet leaned against the gutter. It gave slightly, but silently. She leaned over the edge. This was still an almost two-story drop, but she was directly over where Robert stood on the stairs.

She took aim with her gun, bracing it against her left palm.

"Where is she, cop?"

"She climbed down the cliff on the other side of the house. She's probably found a ride on the road by now."

Robert chuckled and the sound frosted her

spine. "She never climbs down. She's a one-way girl, only going up. Never down. Never lowering herself to street level or willing to descend from her pedestal. She's a full-on empress. Don't you know that? So much higher and grander than the likes of me. And certainly superior to the likes of you, cop.

Another edge of the gutter separated from the roof. Strange that it did so with no noise at all. It felt rubbery against her toes instead of the aluminum she'd expected to feel. She shoved hard against the place where she was leaning, but it didn't move.

"Now I'm going to ask you once again. Once." Robert's voice hardened, as Dani looked down on him again to judge the distance and direction. Laying down her gun, she worked at a couple of bolts holding the area into place. Then she tucked the weapon back into her waistband and leaned forward, gripping the edges of the rubber-like gutter.

"Where is my wife?"

With a push from her feet, Dani flipped over the edge of the roof, holding onto the gutter for everything she was worth and suppressing the terrified screams she wanted to issue. Instead, the gutter gave, again in silence. It lowered her smoothly about eight feet before jerking to a halt. Her hands slipped, hurling her toward Robert who still stood on the steps. Dani straightened her legs, targeting his back.

She connected, shoving him headfirst off the stairs and onto the gravel drive. She landed hard on her back against the stone steps, the back of her head popping against a concrete urn to the right of the stairway. She tried to roll over to stand, but pain shot down to her leg.

Robert grunted as he fell, but he stood and whirled on Dani. Jay butted his head into his stomach and they both went down. Robert's gun skipped from his hand and onto the dirt beside the drive. Jay, in his weakened condition was no match for the man. Dani had to get to the gun first, before Robert. She groaned as she pushed to her knees, but Robert was quicker.

He grabbed the weapon and turned it onto Dani. "Well, now. You have been some trouble, my sweet."

"I'm not your sweet or your wife, and you

know that very well."

"I own you, love. You are whatever I demand that you be." He said the first part several times through their initial romance, but she'd taken it as his dedication to her, his desire for her. How could she have been so blind to his demented definition of love.

Her back spasmed and she flinched and grabbed it crying out in her pain. "You don't understand love, Robert. You need help."

"I need?" He laughed again.

She gripped her own weapon.

"Oh, dear Sammi, I need nothing. I have it all. Money, women, power, respect. I have anything I want." He moved closer to her. "Even you, if I decide you're worth it. Though from the looks of you, I don't think you are."

He leaned over her, gripped her hair and pulled it back to force her chin up. Then he pressed his mouth against hers, his cigar-ridden breath filling her nostrils and coating her lips.

"Stop it." She pushed at him with her empty hand, and pulled her other from behind her.

He laughed again. "Shall I make your

boyfriend watch or just end him right now?"

"No." The word flew out before Dani could bite it back. Robert would've killed Jay anyway, but her concern gave him even more reason.

Jay struggled to his feet. "Why don't you fight a man?"

Robert threw a look in his direction. "Why fight, when I can simply shoot you?" He moved the gun into Jay's direction.

Dani fired. At close range. Directly into his side.

Robert's eyes widened. He moved in slow motion to re-aim his gun at her, but she gathered her strength and shoved him away from her. He fell flat against the gravel drive with a grunt. "You think this is over? This is not over." His voice rasped barely above a whisper.

Dani's pain had escalated, and she still couldn't stand, but she would respond to him. "It's over, Robert. If you don't die now, you'll die in jail or at the end of a needle. Either way, Robert, you're going to die. Are you quite ready for that?"

Jay shuffled toward her. "Are you okay?"

"I hurt my back, but I'll heal." She kept her

eyes on Robert. "You need to sit down."

He shook his head. "Keep your gun on him. Officers are en route, likely state police or FBI."

"Where are you..."

"Cal was hit." He leaned forward and loped toward the side of the house and out of sight. Sirens, which had apparently mingled with the sounds of the night birds and insects, now sang out along this side of the butte.

Robert lifted his head and stared at her. "I would have given you the world."

She didn't want his world. Not an inch of it. "You took my daddy."

He let his head fall back against the rocks with a thump. She couldn't have checked his pulse if she'd wanted to. Keeping the gun trained on him was sapping all of her energy as it was.

Blue and red lights hopped from tree trunk to tree trunk as the sirens abruptly shut off. At least six vehicles approached, the first two were black, unmarked SUV's. Probably FBI or Marshall's office. The first car skidded to a stop in the gravel. The passenger door popped open and a man ordered her to drop her weapon.

Gladly. She released her grip on the gun and let it hang loosely from her fingers as she spread her arms in front of her. Try as she might, she still couldn't sit up. "A police officer is in the back. I think he was shot." Wait, Jay had been shot as well. "There are two of them back there."

Two men in brown uniforms jogged toward the side of the house.

"Lie face down on the ground." The man ordered, still from behind his car door.

"I can't." She pointed at the broken gutter. "I fell from up there."

The standoff lasted only a second longer. The agent closest came to her and took the weapon from her right hand. "Do you have another weapon?"

"No."

"Let's get the paramedics up here." Apparently, the agent was satisfied that she was no longer a threat. "How many people are here?"

"I'm not sure." She started to blurt out the entire story, but paused. "Who are you?"

"I'm asking the questions, ma'am." He didn't sound annoyed, but he wasn't going to allow her any lead from the sound of it.

She tried again. "I don't mean your name, I mean your department."

"FBI." He moved over to allow a paramedic to check her pulse. "Who is responsible for all of this?"

"He is." Dani pointed at the motionless Robert as another team of medics worked over him. "Is there anyone here from the US Marshall's office?"

The man's eyes widened slightly. He'd understood. He put his phone to his cheek and stood, speaking so low even she couldn't hear his words and he was only a few feet from her. He replaced it in his pocket and knelt just below her. "Where is the one in charge?"

That would be Matt, but she'd not seen him. "I don't know."

"Then the secondary?"

Patrick, but he was a turn-coat. McKray was the only other agent she knew. "I don't know that either." A shiver crawled across her shoulders.

"We need a back board over here." The medic called to his teammate who had stepped toward the ambulance.

Dani tried to ignore what that might mean, but

she'd known the chances of her living through that fall were only fifty-fifty. She'd expected to get hurt. Maybe not completely break her back, but her past expectations no longer really mattered. She should have shot Robert from the roof and saved herself the extra pain.

As much as she wished she'd have done that, she couldn't have. Robert would be on her conscience whether he lived or died, but at least she'd done everything she could to stop him before she'd used her gun.

Marji Laine

Jay ground his teeth together against the pain as he stepped out of the hospital elevator.

"Good morning, Sergeant Hunter." A middle-aged nurse who had helped him through his first night smiled at him from behind the counter. "Looks like you didn't take your pain medication this morning."

He didn't like the blurry feeling he got when he used pain meds. "The doc released me to my own recognizance." He gave her a wink. "I'm better than yesterday." Which was true. He'd not even been able to drive here last night, opting instead for a long bus ride.

"Your lady has company." She lifted an eyebrow.

Company? He strode down the antiseptic hallway faster than he should have, encouraging a piercing headache in his left temple. He knocked on the open door before stepping inside. Dani lay in the reclined bed. The purse-lipped grimace on her face turned into a brilliant grin the moment he stepped inside.

Matthew looked out the window with his back to Jay but glanced over his shoulder. "Hunter, I was just saying my goodbyes."

Good.

"I told him that he doesn't have to be a stranger simply because our case is over." Dani looked up at him, her eyebrows raised. Was that expectation she wore in her expression?

"Uh... yeah. Come visit us in Dallas... if you ever get back down that way." But don't go out of your way. As for Jay, he wasn't sure how long he'd stay there, particularly on the Dallas force without Cal.

Matthew chuckled. A strange sound to come from such a stickler of an agent, especially with the groan that came at the end of it. "I'm actually going the other way." He shuffled backward a step and turned slowly. "Heading back to Sacramento. My uncle has a little place out there with some cattle and horses. I'm looking forward to helping him again like I did before I became an agent."

"After you let your injuries heal." Dani shook a finger at him.

And from what Jay understood of his injuries, shot at least twice by Patrick, he would be healing for a while yet.

"I never thanked you for saving my life." Matthew shuffled forward another step and extended his hand. "A medic said if you hadn't found me, stopped the bleeding, I would likely have died before they happened by."

If Jay hadn't needed to use the rock wall for support as he traveled to the back porch, he'd never have found Matthew. The bush into which he'd fallen had almost completely swallowed him. Still, staying with him had been the hardest decision of his life. Jay shook the man's hand. "You're welcome." Although, helping Matthew had kept him from Cal.

"What's the word on your partner." Matthew unknowingly opened the wound a little wider.

The doc had said there was hope, but that was several days ago. "Still in ICU. He's showing some brain activity, but the damage was extensive." The bullet had pierced one of his lungs and done some damage to his liver, but he'd survived five hours of surgery.

"We're keeping him in prayer." Dani covered his hand with her own.

He turned to his girl. "You look as beautiful as ever."

"Liar." She released him, tugged a tissue from the box beside her, and tossed it at his face.

"He's right." Matthew paused at the foot of her bed. "You're not the self-absorbed Sammi Fellows I signed on to protect. Something's different about you. I could tell it when we were sharing that house."

Jay tasted the sting of his words, how the two of them had been married, even in name only. But under such circumstances, their actions certainly could be overlooked.

"When you met me, Matt, I was a church-goer.

You knew that."

The man nodded. "One of the things you had to change in your life. No photography and no regular church attendance."

"Right. So, I started reading Scripture on my own, and... I found my faith. I can't wait to go back to church, now, but my faith isn't there. It's in the God of the Bible and in His Son, Jesus Christ. The rules disallowing me to go to church actually helped me remember that, because they forced me to find the Lord in other ways. And He came to me because I looked for Him."

Matthew had been quiet. Hard to tell if the agent was being polite or truly interested.

"He came to you because you looked for Him?" The man's brows ruffled. "I confess, I don't get that."

A genuine smile spread across her face. "You will, Matt. Look for Him. Here." She took a Gideon Bible from the drawer beside her and held it out to him. "Read about Him, and ask Him to reveal His truth to you. He will. He even says, 'Faith comes from hearing and hearing from the Word of God.'"

A soft look came over the agent's eyes. He

took the book from her. "Okay. I'll read. And I'll ask Him to show Himself."

"Start in the book of John."

"John, got it." He reached down and squeezed her toes. "Take care of yourself, Sam... uh... Dani." He turned to Jay. "You, too."

Jay patted his back as he stepped toward the door. "May the Lord bless you." Why those words came out of his mouth, he couldn't say. They hadn't been planned.

Matthew hesitated and cast a glance his direction. "Thanks." He held Jay's gaze a moment and then turned for the door.

He made a painfully slow exit, but most men wouldn't be standing after the punishment Matthew's body had taken between bullets and surgery. Not after only a week in the hospital.

Jay faced Dani and noticed a wispy look in her eyes. "He'll be all right."

"I believe you." She ran her finger under her nose and sniffed. "First time I ever heard him the least bit interested in God. I hope he finds his answers."

"He will if he listens with a sincere heart." Of

course, she already knew that. She'd said something to that affect when they were enjoying some regular dates last spring. "You have a sincere heart." Stifling a groan, he tugged a chair close to her bedside and reached for her hand.

"How's your shoulder?" She gave his hand a squeeze. "I was surprised the doctor discharged you yesterday."

"Once my blood levels evened out, I was fine." Fine being relative. "Still a little sore."

"A little... Yeah, right. I don't see how you're even functioning."

He shrugged his good shoulder. "What is the doctor saying." At least her back hadn't been broken.

"He's talking discharge. Maybe tomorrow if I can start walking a little farther. He wants to make sure the disk that slipped stays in line after the swelling is all gone."

Her poor back must be black and blue and purple. Not something he wanted to see. "You saved my life."

"Not a bit of it, Jay Hunter. We stopped Robert. That was the goal."

Permanently. Jay didn't like anyone to die, but he couldn't mourn the man who had caused so much pain to so many.

"Matt told me that the other two agents are fine, knocked out with some type of gas, but Robert's organization is completely gone, now. With Tony D. and Patrick on their way to jail and Robert dead, there's no one left to try to recreate his mess.

Jay nodded. "Thankfully, most of the women and children had been released and treated last year when you took him down."

"I didn't do that." The slight smile dropped from her face. "You know what I did." She looked at the sheet half covering her.

"Dani, you made mistakes. So have I. So have we all. That just confirms you're as fallen and in need of forgiveness as everyone else." He released her hand and stroked the side of her face. "But you need to find a way to forgive yourself."

"Can you forgive me?"

The guilt and remorse in her eyes broke his heart. "Dani, I love you." He kissed her forehead. "Nothing can change that. Certainly nothing in your past." He kissed her lips, keeping his touch gentle for his own benefit as well as hers. She responded, reaching her arm around his neck, but halted with a painful whimper.

"Oh, sweetheart." He collected her hand and cupped her cheek with his other one. "Let yourself heal."

She settled back into the extra pillows that supported her. "I'm not sure where to go when the doctor does release me."

"Have you spoken to Tasha?"

"She wants me to come back to Dallas, of course, but I won't have a job or any support now that I'm no longer in witness protection." She shut her eyes. "I don't even know what name I should go by."

"That I can help you with." His face probably looked downright goofy, but with the danger finally gone, he felt certain she would accept his proposal. She probably wouldn't appreciate receiving it here in the hospital, though.

"Oh, really?" She lifted her eyebrows in mock innocence. "And how do you pro... expect to do that?" Her cheeks pinked slightly.

He stroked her fingers lightly and studied her hand. "With a ring. For this finger." With only a little strain against his injury, he kissed her finger. "And if I thought I could get up, I'd get down on one knee right now."

She giggled. Actually giggled. "Oh, please don't. I don't want to see you in pain. Not again. Ever."

He sobered. "Part of the job, baby."

"None of this has been part of your job." She traced her hand lightly across his shoulder. "This has been my fault. My past. My present."

"No. Not anymore." He clasped her hand in his good one and pressed a kiss onto her knuckles. "That is, neither your present nor your future. Not if I have anything to say about it."

She positively glowed. "Are you sure?"

Was she kidding? "Absolutely. And we'll make things official when we get back. If... that is, assuming you're agreeable?" He sucked in a breath.

Her left eyebrow raised like it always did when she was teasing with him. "I'll have to hear the terms first."

The look she gave was intoxicating. He

smothered his smile and stood, leaning closer to hover near her lips. "Well, you would be required to commit to this... agreement... making the necessary promises to cement your devotion."

"Hmm. I'm tempted. Is there a... completion date... to this agreement?"

"Nope." He stroked her cheek with the back of his hand. "This is permanent."

"Everlasting?" Her whisper warmed his lips, enticing him.

"Exactly." He brushed her lips with his own. "Think you can handle that?"

"I do."

"It's time."

Dani stepped aside to let Carla Reid lead the way down the flower-lined pathway of the Dallas Arboretum. Her tea-length dress swayed slightly as she took the turn beyond the high, flowering hedges blocking her view of the gathering. Jay's sister, Kristi blew her a kiss and then followed Carla.

Tasha gave her a grin. The navy of the dress

made her eyes sparkle. "You've got this." She lifted a bouquet of Shasta daisies and started her slow walk to the corner.

Dani watched her friend for a moment, thankful for her generosity while Dani settled back into some sort of normalcy. She ran a hand down her white gown, satin with a chiffon overlay like those of her bridesmaids. It reached almost to her ankles, and the simple design matched her. Well, it matched her now.

"Go ahead." The wedding coordinator that Carla had insisted on hiring had done an amazing job and made all of the decisions so easy.

She took her first steps, memories of the last year flooding her. "Oh, Daddy, I wish you were here. You were so right. About everything." She squeezed her eyes tight for a nano-second. No crying. Her groom deserved to see her at her best, not weepy and red-faced.

At least the minister wouldn't be calling out her hated name. Her best decision since she'd accepted Jay's proposal was to legally change her name. She wouldn't discard her family name, but never more would she be called *Sammi* or

Samantha Fellows. Danielle hadn't been her choice of names when Matt assigned it, but it had grown on her. Especially the way Jay said it.

She made the turn and grinned into the faces of the loved ones standing before her. Matt hadn't made it for the wedding, but his card had wished them both God's blessings and promised his prayers for them. Wow. She continued to pray that the Lord would keep drawing him closer, but it sounded like he'd become a believer.

Members of the church—she'd loved being able to engage in a fellowship again—filled most of the chairs that had been set out. Jay's large, extended family filled the rest, and everyone turned to smile at her.

She tried to get a glimpse of Jay through the group, but couldn't find him. Ty and Jay's younger brother, Kyle, both beamed at her from the steps of the raised dais. Cal leaned on a stool on the stage itself, closer to where the minister stood. Over six months of rehab had done wonders, but the man still had weak spells. He would never be a cop again, but he didn't seem to mind. Especially when he posted pictures of the catches from his brother's lake on social media.

Then Jay himself stepped to the head of the aisle, grinning at her. Even so early in the spring, his natural, Native American tan were accented by his brilliant white teeth. And his dark eyes held such love. He stepped toward her and took her hand into the crook of his elbow until they reached the front row. She paused and pulled a rose from her bouquet. Handing it to Jay's mom, she bent and planted a kiss on her cheek.

Once again slipping her hand onto his arm, she walked with him up to the pastor. No, she didn't deserve this amazing man, but God was good. And she would do everything she could to make the rest of his life full of joy and love.

About the Author

Marji Laine has completed seventeen years of homeschooling with the surreal notion that she'll now have time on her hands. But that's unlikely. Her publishing company, Write Integrity Press, keeps her extremely busy. In her spare time, she teaches a high school and college Bible Study, leads a Sunday morning high school fellowship group, directs a children's choir, and sings in her church's adult choir.

She enjoys road trips with her family and friends, photography, scrapbooking, and participating in musical theater. Her favorite past time is game night with her family and her kids' extended collection of friends.

You can stay updated on Marji's books through her newsletter.

Sign up at her webpage: MarjiLaine.com.

From the Author

Dear Reader,

It's hard to believe that Dani's saga is over. Wow. These characters have become so special to me. I'm not sure I can let them go quite yet.

So, while Dani's "saga" is over and her secrets have all been revealed, I do have one more plan for Dani and Jay. Sort of a "honeymoon" story. Yes, that's actually an excellent description!

Due to my responsibilities with my publishing company, I'm unable to write as often as I'd like, but I hope to get Dani's honeymoon story (wait until you see where Jay takes her!) completed and out to you soon.

Speaking of my publishing company, I'm reminded constantly of Ephesians 3:20, that the Lord is able to do more than we can ask or imagine. He certainly did that when He placed me in this wonderful company. I'm profoundly thankful to so many of the authors who constantly keep me in their prayers and continue to encourage me! They are not only outstanding writers; they are amazing ladies!

I'm also so very grateful to some special people who helped me work through this book. Thank you to my intern, Brittany, who is learning this business in great leaps and bounds. Her eyes on my first draft were invaluable! And also thanks to my final reader, Breana Clubine. I so appreciate your view and your encouragement! And lastly, I want to thank my road trip buddy, Lill Kohler, who urged me to visit Abilene in person and not just on internet sites. Thanks so much for traveling road by road with me to find just the right settings for my story, and thanks for sharing your views of this city you have visited so often!

And thank you to you, dear readers, for staying on me! For sharing your enthusiasm over Dani's story and keeping her high on my priority list! I'm so delighted that her secrets are no longer a burden to her.

But I think she still has a few more pieces of trouble ahead of her!

Until then, be blessed. Follow Christ. And keep reading!

Sincerely,

Marji

P.S. If you enjoyed Grime & Punishment, please consider returning to the Amazon page and leaving a review! Doing so is the NICEST thing you can do for an author!

Other Books from Marji Laine

Grime Fighter Mysteries
A Complete Series!

Working as a crime scene cleaner is perfect for neat-nick Dani Foster who has recently been relocated by her witness security contact. But she can't hide the investigative reactions drilled into her by her detective father. Even though her discoveries, and the explorations they instigate, often put her into funny, uncomfortable, and sometimes dangerous positions.

Marji Laine

Heath's Point Suspense
COUNTER POINT – Book 1

Her dad's gone. Her business is in trouble, and her car's in the lake. Cat McPHerson doesn't have anything else to lose… except her life. And a madman is determined to take that.

Her former boyfriend, Ray Alexander, returns as a hero from his foreign mission, bringing back death-threats. Cat must find a way to trust Ray, the man who broke her heart or neither of them will survive.

BREAKING POINT – Book 2
Why would anyone want her dead?

Alynne Stone wanted nothing to do with her parents' inn after they left their lifelong home in Dallas to move to Heath's Point, Texas. Then an emergency phone call not only drew her to her parents' bed and breakfast, it thrust her into the crosshairs of a killer.

Lieutenant Jason Danvers has no idea why his kind and generous friend was killed. But the man's beautiful, prodigal daughter needs all the help he can give her to stay alive.

AIN'T MISBEHAVING

Book 1 of the
Dallas Duets Clean Billionaire Romance Series

Annalee Chambers: Poised, wealthy, socially elite. Convict.

She floated through life in a pampered, crystal bubble until she smashed it with a single word. Dealing with the repercussions of that word might break her, ruin her family, and land her in jail. That is, unless a handsome worker from the "other" side of the tracks, who has secrets of his own, can help her find her way.